I0748407

THE LEOPARD OF ELIOT HOUSE

IHEANYI ANUNUSO

HANYVISION

UNITED KINGDOM/ UNITED STATES/ NIGERIA

Copyright ©2022 By Iheanyi Anunuso

All Rights Reserved.

ISBN - 978-1-7397772-3-4

Acknowledgement

I would like to thank my parents Prof Clifford Anunuso and Lady Catherine Anunuso (KSC).

The personal sacrifices they have made for my siblings and I whilst not always appreciated in our younger days, is the reason we made it as far as we have. Hopefully, they are proud of this work, an attestation that yet another generation pursues new boundaries of excellence and achievement.

I would like to thank Lorna McCracken, my workplace manager turned advisor, for her ceaseless encouragement to finish this work, despite all the distractions of this Covid-inhibited time.

Finally, I would like to thank Timothy Driscoll of the Harvard Library. When I flew over to Boston before the pandemic, I'd never been there before and didn't know a soul. I took the train down to Harvard Yard in Cambridge and hoped for the best. I was lucky to have met you that day, and the resources that you found for me on Chris Ohiri and the time you dedicated to help me were invaluable, and without which, this work could not have truly been done. God Bless you and yours.

PROLOGUE

Uzoma Chukwuka walked through Harvard Yard, an extremely proud young man. He had secured admission into the oldest and most distinguished University in the United States, the same one his parents had attended and met before eventually getting married to each other after leaving.

His father, the Nigerian born Uchechi, and his mother, the quintessential New England beauty Mary, were accompanying him to help drop off his things at the Greenough hostel, the same hostel his dad had stayed in, some two decades prior.

Mary was excited that he had made it, something she had wanted for him when they had returned to Boston when he was still a baby, but she had always been careful to make sure she wasn't pushing too hard to steer him in that direction. She didn't really need to. His Dad never failed to remind him to never take opportunities for granted, citing the circumstances he grew up in back in Nigeria.

Uzoma didn't mind the gentle but firm encouragement from his dad, something he seemed to understand even though he hadn't really lived in Nigeria, aside from a few months holiday visits on occasion. His bond with his father was something that had always been present for him. Even though he had largely grown up in New England, he could still speak Igbo quite well, the native language of the largest group in Eastern Nigeria, where he could trace his lineage from.

But his father had been strangely quiet during the trip from Boston, the opposite of his mum, who had tried unsuccessfully to his amusement, in hiding her excitement. And now, he noticed his dad wander off from the entrance like he was looking for something…or someone.

"Is Dad feeling alright?" He asked his Mum, to which she looked towards her husband quizzically, and then a veil of understanding seemed to come over her face, and she turned to her Harvard freshman son.

"Your Dad's fine, honey…It's just been a while since he's been here. C'mon, let's get you set up in Greenough!"

"Maybe he's already bored, just like I am." Uzoma turned towards his twelve-year-old sister, who he had almost forgotten had come on the trip and had been thankfully quiet. Until now.

"Oh, please shut up, Ada. It's been a great day so far. We don't need you spoiling it."

"Alright, you two." Mary called out from the back of the car. "There will be no silliness on the Yard. Now, someone come help me unpack."

They all joined her in bringing Uzoma's stuff down from the car, including Uchechi who immediately engaged Ada in their favourite game of wrestling to the amusement of everyone.

Once Uzoma's things had been sorted out, they decided to have a small drive around the campus to see what Uchechi and Mary could remember from their university days, looking at restaurants and fast-food joints around the Yard, until Mary asked Uchechi to take them to the football stadium for Harvard University.

The place seemed to look as magnificent as Mary remembered it, and she led Ada on a sightseeing chase around the grounds of the famous stadium. Uzoma's Dad meanwhile, solemnly beckoned to his son and led him to a less impressive field just across the road, which was surrounded by a metal fence.

"I'm sorry, I didn't seem engaged when we first arrived." Uchechi said to his son, as they walked along the side of the encircled pitch. "It's been almost 20 years since I was last here in Cambridge, walking around Harvard Yard. It was a great place for me to school and learn what America was truly about.

But it also holds one very sad memory for me. A friend I lost a long time ago. An exceptional student and one of the greatest men anyone would have had the chance to meet. He was Igbo, just like you and me, but he will always be remembered for being so much more, and this soccer field is named in his honour so that those memories never die.

Let me tell you the story of the way I got here, and about a great man and friend…

CHAPTER ONE

June 1959

Coming home from school with my friends in the afternoon sun, the same group of us whom have walked together on this same path for the last couple of years now. An attention-grabbing group we were. Laughing, talking, arguing, and then laughing again. Its 2 pm, by which time most schools in Owerri are closed...Translation? girls are out of school and on the streets, on their way home.

Of course, most of the boys out there were just simply glad that school is over, and that we could go out and play as much football as we wanted. But the facts were that 1950's Nigeria was quite conservative, and as a teenager, the only time that you could speak quite freely with anyone of the opposite sex, was outside of the earshot of anyone outside of your age group that you didn't know.

Thus the usual excitement and hum of activity, as boys tried to get the attention of the girls and make small talk to introduce themselves on the chance that it would be the beginning of a relationship.

My group was not much different to the other boys. Now that I think of it, all the enthusiastic noisemaking was generally to draw the attention of the girls that we liked and wanted to talk to.

The closest friend I had in the group was also my current neighbour, Emeka, whom I had known for years long before my family had moved into the area we lived in now, going back through primary school. It was only when we started living in the area, that we found out that our families knew each other going back two generations.

The rest of the gang were, Chidi, I.K, Obi and Kachi, all of whom I came to know from going to the schools, living in the same area or through the various shared interests and social clubs that our parents were involved in, which was usually the case in a town like Owerri, where everybody knew everyone else or someone that knew them.

Every one of us though was especially happy today because, mother's younger brother James, was coming home today on a visit from the United States, where he had been living for the past five years, in New York to be precise.

From his letters home, he had been describing a truly remarkable country, the size, the different groups of people, the infrastructure, fashion trends and of course, the cars, especially when he starts talking about the fast ones (he loved the Shelby but was generally interested in cars because he studied Mechanical Engineering in University.)

Sadly though, these were not the only things that he wrote about. You see, he lived in New York where it can be quite cold for most of the year, and his ideal choice would have been to live in the southern part of the U.S, where the climate is much warmer, just like it is here in Nigeria.
But, because of the stories that we had heard about the happenings that occurred in the deep south of the country because of the de-segregation movement, no one could guarantee, least of all him, his safety, and so it became a big issue before he could leave, and it was decided that he would have to have to school and live in one of the more urbane areas of the country such as Chicago, New York or Los Angeles.

Los Angeles was immediately struck out by the family as being far out, and so he was left with the option of either New York or Chicago, of which he chose the former as he had heard so much of the city.

He would have obviously liked to live in LA.-movie star land- but it was the family footing the bill for his travel and school fees, as he was unable to secure a scholarship, as well as putting up the money he would need to keep well until he settled down.

However, his recent letters have been describing a social phenomenon that had been increasing in recent years. These stories which I alluded to earlier had to do with the African American population in the country- the Africans who had been the victims of the slave trade, about which we were taught in school.
These people still after all these years seemed still to be regarded as second-class citizens and had been victims of some unbelievably horrific attacks on their homes and persons, without any seeming protection of the law there.

Uncle James though, says that the people behind these attacks were a minority and were generally more prominent in the deep southern parts of the United States, like Mississippi and Georgia, which was why it was seen by the family and friends that as a Black man himself, hc was not to live in such areas.

There however was a movement in the country, led by a Martin Luther King, which seemed to comprise of a lot of people from different cultural backgrounds, blacks, whites, Jews all coming together to form a coalition to express their desire to put an end to the unequal treatment that was so unfair and against the principles on which the United States was founded.

The movement had been marching around the country in the face of intimidation and had been growing in numbers, and this coalition was looking like it were about to really bring about change in the country.

These were some of the reasons that I was so happy that Uncle James was coming home, so that I could ask how things were going with the movement.
More importantly though, and the reason why all my friends were coming to my house was the gifts that Uncle James would be coming back with, you know, those new fashion clothing that he kept writing about- jeans or denim he called them-, shoes, hopefully some nice smelling perfume, (cheap, but who cared or knew).

Usually, depending on how much that an individual could afford, most Africans

brought back a lot when they visited from overseas as gifts, for the people they knew at home.
My friends, naturally, hoped for some consideration in the homecoming bounty.

For me however, apart from all that I had previously stated about my interest in my uncle's visit, there was one secret reason that I was extremely happy about.
I had decided against all my father's wishes, that I was not going to study in Nigeria for my University education.

I, Uchechi Chukwuka, wanted to go and study halfway around the world in California, and I needed Uncle James to help me convince my family.

•

I was the first-born son of my parents, Henry and Akunna Chukwuka, a significant role in many families and cultures, but, even more in my culture.
We were Igbos (sometimes pronounced Ibo), a proud African Ethnic group, which live east of the river Niger, in Nigeria, a British colony that was on the path to independence, as were a host of African countries in the year 1959.

Being a first-born son was especially important in my family, where my parents believed that I should set a good example for the rest of my family, that is, my four brothers and sister.
That meant taking the harshest of the collective punishment when there were problems like fights between us siblings, or, when I did not obey instructions like we taught to like, not staying out late or, being told not to go to certain places.

The logic, and quite rightly so as I was to discover later, was that your first child was usually the first role model that the rest of your children used as an example.
As much as parents could be outstanding characters, sometimes, kids look to people they can relate to more easily.

My father Henry and I, looked alike to a remarkable extent, we were about the same height, liked and disliked almost the same fruits and food, and walked with the same gait.
We were also both independent minded and short-tempered, which was a bit of a toxic combination for most of my teenage years, tinged by my discoveries and rebellion, and

led to numerous clashes throughout that period.
Henry Chukwuka was a very educated and accomplished man. He had studied Industrial Chemistry at University in England, which was the only way you could study at the time back in the forties, as there were no universities in Nigeria in those colonial days.
This was not easy to do at the time, because of the expense involved, travel, school fees and boarding, and especially because my grandfather Iheanyi, was a palm wine tapper (this involved climbing palm trees and drawing the wine). It was dangerous and did not get you a lot of money.

That combined with having to live for several years away from your family, in a far-away country that was completely different from the one you grew up in, and fend for yourself, made it an extremely difficult preposition.

It did help that our village put money together to help him, as he was the first to show a real interest in school and they were proud of him.

Henry Chukwuka went through all the logistic, cultural and financial barriers and came through with excellent results and won the admiration of everyone who knew him, including my mom, who knew him before he left but was not allowed by her family to go abroad to study but went instead to the newly created University of Ife, graduating with distinction in Journalism herself.

My father had high expectations for me, both academically and in terms of being able to set a good standard for my siblings to follow, and when he thought that I wasn't living up to my potential at any given time, he let loose.

He seemed to forget that men were boys who grew up later.

Despite all our arguments, and though I never said it, I was proud of my father. I liked the way people listened to him and respected his views on issues. I liked how people looked at me differently when they realised that I was his son and thought that I was of a certain intellectual and moral standard just because of the fact.

Sometimes I wished he knew how proud I was to be his son, how I truly respected him, and yearned for that level of respect that he got in whatever he did or said.

In that period of my life, I wanted to prove to him and everyone that I could accomplish the things that he did, and I thought the only way of doing that was to follow the path that he had blazed.
That way, I could establish my independence and at the same time gain the respect that I wanted from my parents, while providing that example to my younger siblings that everyone was talking about.

I guess I was just a young adult growing up in a newly independent country, I wanted to do everything, see everywhere, no limits attached.

I was under no illusions that this was going to be easy. I had no money, no job, and would need something substantial to get me on my way.
Getting Uncle James on my side was crucial I thought, to convincing my family about the idea.

The timing of his visit could not have been any better.

•

The crucial meeting was held on a Friday evening around 8 pm. The timing was important because of the critical nature of the discussion taking place. Everything needed to be done just right.

The time at which James and I wanted to talk to my father was deliberate. First, Friday evening was the end of the work week, with the entire weekend to look forward to.

Henry was an administrator with overall responsibility at one of the Eastern region's (Nigeria was made up of three regions at the time, the others being north and west) biggest palm plantations which was close to our town Owerri.
It was a Monday to Friday, 7:30am to 3:30pm job, for which he had to travel about an hour to and from every day. He liked his job; he had been with the regional palm plantation authority for six years now and had gradually risen to the top.

But, with all the normal stress that comes with responsibility over the actions of others, deadlines, and targets, he needed his relaxation period after work.
This was how James and I arrived at Friday, 8pm, being our D-day.

We came down from my room upstairs, where we had been and preparing, raising and answers among ourselves of the type we thought my dad might ask.

Henry was just finishing his last glass of palm wine, one of the benefits of running a palm plantation-a weekly quota of free and fresh stock.

James said, “Good morning, Henry. How was your day”?

“Oh, just the usual day at work, making sure that proper procedures and standards are maintained, that everyone is doing their best to keep us on schedule, especially the palm wine tappers who are difficult to monitor because they work in the vast plantations.”

“I caught two of them sleeping with a small Jerri can of palm wine beside them. But since it was only the first time, I had seen them, I let them off with a stern warning.”

“And... its Friday, which brings the best and most enjoyable part of the job… taking home my regular Friday palm wine quota.”

This last bit said while gently tapping the now half empty bottle of palm wine and laughing with James.

“Good evening papa” I said.

“Evening Uchechi, and by the way James, would you want to finish this bottle with me.”

“Sure, free and fresh, what’s not to like about such an offer, if only everything else in life was that forthcoming.”

“You already sound like you’ve had a few drinks” said dad laughing.

“Papa, could I have a glass as well.”

“Well, its fresh and so I think it will be alright.”

You see, palm wine is non-alcoholic, and, has a nice, sweet taste to it when its fresh, but the longer it stays after it has been drawn from the palm tree, the more the taste turns sour, which in turn increases its potency. This happens as result of the yeast in the wine fermenting and thereby boosting the alcohol content.

So, with a glass of palm wine each, James and I sat down across the room from my dad, facing him. Sensing that we wanted to talk about something, my father, always direct, said,

"Ok, I don't think the two of you left your card games upstairs to talk about my work procedures and news, so you might as well come out with whatever it is you want to talk about."
"Fine..., Papa, I want to study mechanical engineering in university when I finish secondary school in a few months' time...."

"Fantastic! My son, that's the direction that this country is headed in with all the infrastructure that will be needed in Nigeria, once we become independent from the British in a short time, by the Grace of God."

"In America," said James.

"WHAT!"

"I heard about this school" I said quickly, "It's called U.C.L.A., a very good school and they encourage students who are good in sports by giving them scholarships."

My dad loved sports very much, especially football. He was quite good at it and had played in central midfield for one of the best amateur teams during his youth.

"Where is UCLA?" Henry Chukwuka asked. "What does the acronym stand for?"

"It stands for University of California, Los Angeles" James answered, deciding it was best to get straight to the heart of the matter.

"Los Angeles? On the West coast of America?"

My tongue seemed to dry and in capable of speech at that moment, as all the possible ways in which this conversation could go wrong, ran through my mind's eye. However, a tiny recess of my brain was registering the fact that my father had seemingly forgotten to register any strong opposition to the fact that I was requesting to go abroad to study, and to America no less.

A gradual sense of optimism that there might be hope for my dream of a student life in America, began to flicker. But they were going to be hurdles, especially with my choice of coast...

“You can’t be serious” My dad said, turning to me. “If we didn’t think it was a good choice to send James out that far, why do you think your mother and I would let you go that there? By the way, where’s your mother? Akunna!” He called out “Come and listen to what your son is saying. via James.” The last few words delivered with a quick side-eye to his brother-in-law, who shifted uncomfortably for the first time.

“What’s the matter Uchechi?” My mom asked, as she came into view, with a pensive expression on her face.

She was an exceptionally beautiful woman who only seemed to grow more beautiful as the years rolled by. She was from the most populous cultural subgroup in Igbo culture, called Mbaise (the 5-nation people). They were a very industrious and determined people and envied by most other people for the way they always seemed to stick together and stand up for one another, which wasn’t always a noted trait among the Igbo, the most republican and independent of any tribe in the history of Africa, and the world.

My mum was a proud journalist, one of the golden generation of scribes at the forefront of the independence movement that had been successfully sweeping through the continent of Africa over the last five years. She had designs on working with one of the national newspapers in the capital city, Lagos, just like the founder of the first national daily, and current President of Nigeria, Nnamdi Azikiwe, who through his newspaper and later, his political party the NCNC, lead the independence movement from Great Britain.

However, when my dad received the job to run the Research & Development Department at the Ministry of Agriculture for the government of the then Eastern Region of Nigeria, which would be run out of Owerri, she instead set her sights on establishing the first female run newspaper in the region, understanding that this was an opportunity for the newly married couple to strongly begin building the foundations of their own family right away, which would free them from the rigours of uncertainty, serving as a springboard for even more ambitious goals down the road, especially that Dream newspaper that she and Henry talked so much about.

Mothers and their first sons always have a special bond, as do fathers and their first daughters, and my mum and I were not any different. Convincing her that her first son, moving thousands of miles away to study in a place where she had heard many disturbing stories about, was a good idea, would be a truly difficult task, Uchechi thought as his mum's eyes met his.

"Uchechi is planning to go abroad to study in the US, alongside James" announced my dad.

"Is this true, Uche?" My mum asked, to which I nodded affirmatively, still trying mentally to loosen my tongue.

"Do you have anything to do with this, James?" She asked with a sharp accusing look in his direction.

"No, Akunna. This has all been Uchechi's idea, and he has dreamt of doing that for a while. He only came to me to find out how it was like to live there from day to day, and the options available to him."

"And you didn't deem it fit to let us know about these future aspirations of his?" My dad enquired.

"That's why we are here, brother" James answered, to which everyone in the room, turned towards Uchechi, waiting for him to address them all on these overseas plans of his.

•

Uchechi climbed into bed quietly, turning down the lantern as he did. He lay down motionless for a while, looking up at the ceiling and oblivious to the usually annoying sound of the mosquitoes flying around in his room, looking for an opening to bite.

The music of E.T Mensah wafted through his open window, coming from a distance away in the night air. There was a party going on somewhere he thought, but as he listened to the highlife melody of "Pom-Pom," tears streamed down his face.

He had dreamt so much of going to America over the past few months. All the stories he knew of that land, all the places he wanted to see and people he dreamt every night of meeting...everything seemed as far away and remote a real possibility as it was, for the first time since he's very first dream about God's own country.

"I have no money for you to school in America right now" Henry Chukwuka quietly told the assembled group in his living room." I can see it is something that you want very much" he continued, as everyone looked at Uchechi's stoic but crestfallen face.

"I must think about the rest of your brothers and sister as well, and plan for them. There is no conceivable way, that I could pay for your education over in America on my income, never mind the transport costs and your upkeep until you find a way to support yourself.
I too, went abroad to study. I know what I had to go through to not only survive being in a foreign country where I knew no one, but to study at the highest levels of education and excel. I've told you a lot of stories about my time there, but I can never truly describe the experience to you in full. There are just things that you can only understand if you experience them for yourself."

Uchechi sat in silence as his dad spoke. He would catch the concerned eye of his mum on occasion, and that of his uncle, but he tried to avoid betraying the sheer amount of sadness going through his entire body as he listened to his father.

He had always had the reputation of keeping his thoughts and feelings to himself. Known as “the quiet one” to friends and family, it had always been his character. He kept a small circle of friends, and an even smaller circle of girlfriends, or to be accurate, none.

His quiet disposition did not lend itself much to the attention of girls in the full bloom of their teen years, especially the ones that he desired. His friends always told him, that the reason that he always he kept falling for the “bad girls” in his school and in the neighbourhood, was only because he was quiet, or so they read, in books about relationships.

Be that as it may, he never could work up the courage to talk to the girls. They were usually popular or/and pretty, and always drew a crowd, something else which was an anathema to Uchechi’s being. The perfect time, when he could get a word to a girl, he liked without anyone else around, never seemed to materialise...

“The only way you can study abroad is if someone will sponsor you, just like I was. I was very lucky that the village saw my potential and came together to put in the money that enabled me to go abroad to England and study. We don't live in a village now. Owerri is a much bigger town, attracting people from different parts of the Eastern Region, as well as the rest of the country. People don't come together in the way that they used to when I was younger. Everyone has their goals, mostly individual, to survive and make it in the big city, and in turn, uplift the rest of their families in the rural areas. Coming together to uplift individuals in the town, is as rare a thing now as rainfall in January. If there is anyone that would sponsor you, I could think about letting you go abroad. But I know it is almost impossible because of the costs involved. Anyone that would sponsor you would not only have to fly you over there, but they would also have to get the universities that would accept African students."

"You see" Uchechi's dad continued, gesticulating towards James, "I'm sure your uncle has told you about the social upheavals going on in America; the riots, the racism and the protests which the African-American population have embarked on in the last few years. They have only started desegregating the schools in the South.

“It’s only a problem in the South” James interjected, receiving a stern look from Henry in return, but continuing, nonetheless. “The ones that Uchechi and I were looking at are in the Northeast and in the West. The racial bias isn’t as pronounced there as it is in the South.”

“Well,” Henry continued, still giving James one last frown as he turned back towards his son, “All I’m doing is to let you know the obstacles facing you if you decide to embark on this quest. I know your mother and I would prefer it if you to go to university here, especially to the great new University of Nigeria, Nsukka that has just been established, giving our people their first university in this region of the country. But more importantly, you are our first child, and we would miss you terribly.”

There had been an awkward silence for a few seconds, as Uchechi looked up at his parents quietly and saw a sad look on his mother’s face, but would never forget the look he had seen on his father’s face, coupled with the sad note in his voice that made his ears prick up a few seconds before...

"I've also lived abroad too, and I can tell you it isn't as easy as it appears to be. You can ask your mum, and if your uncle is truthful, he too would probably tell you some of the jobs he's had to do to keep himself together.
I don't want to stop you from pursuing your dream, I just want you to know the reality of the way things are and will be. There isn't money to pay for your school abroad. We can barely afford to support your Uncle James in America, it has been a massive undertaking from me, your mum, and the rest of her family, and we are eagerly awaiting the results admirably showing the fruits of our labour...."

This last sentence was said with a quiet look in the direction of James, who smiled and shifted uncomfortably in his chair.

"Again, my son, even though my wish is to see you school here rather than expose you to the problems of a world far from ours, I wouldn't stop you if there was a chance you could go without the financial and logistical hindrances I've mentioned. But alas..."

•

As Uchechi's eyes grew heavy with sleep, strains of E.T Mensah's "Ghana Freedom" floated into his room, with whoops of joys accompanying the track from the revellers, perfectly encapsulating the one thought in Uchechi's head.

Freedom.

A desire of freedom from the constraints of his environment. A desired freedom to pursue his dream to see the world, and be everything he wanted to be...

But how?

CHAPTER TWO

"Beautiful. Just beautiful" remarked David as the Peugeot Station Wagon sped down the dusty road on its way to Owerri from Enugu. He was looking at miles of tall, beautiful palm trees as far as the eye could see, across the horizon. A major source of income for the predominately Igbo people of Eastern Nigeria, their silhouette, matched against the clear blue sky was inescapable across the land.

David Henry was in great spirits that morning and had been ever since he's Pan American airlines flight touched down in Lagos a few weeks earlier, welcomed at the airport by an aide from his esteemed host, the Nigerian Minster of Education, Stephen Awokoya…

•

David, the Director of Admissions at the most prestigious American institution of learning, Harvard University, had come to West Africa with a small group of admissions directors from elite American universities; Brown and Amherst amongst others; seeking to make an American contribution to what was the dawning of a new era on the African continent.

The late 1950's and early 1960's saw a wave of territories on the continent starting from Ghana in West Africa, begin to declare independence from the colonial powers of Great Britain, France and Belgium.

It was the culmination of events that could be traced back to the end of World War II in 1945, as enlisted Black African soldiers, often ignored and forgotten by history for their immeasurable sacrifices and contributions to the defeat of Nazi Germany and Japan, returned to their various hometowns and villages. In all the time that the Europeans had arrived on the continent since the 15th century on the back of the slave trade, African men and women had never lived in close quarters with their European counterparts.

This had contributed to the "mystique" of the White man, as they were referred to by the Indigenous African people sometimes, or truthfully, most of the time in those early days. The technologically superior Europeans dazzled their hosts with their advancements. Guns, and bicycles later, examples of things previously unseen on the continent, which enhanced the mystique of the visitors, especially as they never really lived in close quarters.

The Second World War changed all that, even more than the First one, which African men, again unheralded and unrecognised, also fought for the allies.
Battle conditions meant that for the first time, and in great numbers, men of African origin and their European counterparts lived and fought in close quarters, allowing the former to see their fellow soldiers live their lives and suffer as much as them, doing all the regular things that all men did; eat, bathe, fight and die; just the way they and all the people they knew back home, went through life's struggles.

This experience was eye opening for the African men fighting that war so much so that when they returned home from that tragic war in the latter part of 1945, they passed on that knowledge to their family and friends back home, gradually eroding the mystique that the European men had for centuries, and calling into question why men who were exactly like them, should rule over them in their own land, birthing the independence movement that would consume the continent fifteen years later. It was that atmosphere, that David and his group of American University administrators met on their arrival in late 1959.

The aide to the Minister along with a security detail of three policemen, helped David and the rest of the team secure their luggage and transfer into the waiting vehicles provided for the visiting team on the instructions of the Minister, as logistical help to enable them carry out the purpose of their expedition.

The Peugeot Station Wagons made their way through the Lagos streets to the Ikeja Arms Inn, the best hotel in Lagos at the time and the preferred place of residence for David and the rest of the team. They were fascinated by their view of the city as they sped past the buildings, street side markets large and small, and of course the street vendors that approached the cars anytime they were held up at an intersection with all sorts of wares ranging from groundnuts and bananas to fresh bread. It was the first time anyone in the group had visited Nigeria, and along with the humidity they had felt as soon as they stepped off the plane, they soaked in the sights and sounds of Africa's

largest and most populous city as they made their way towards their hotel.
They got to the hotel around 5pm, with the entire party looking forward to their beds as their journey to Africa's most populous country had begun at 9am the previous day, on Thursday. The flight from New York, where the party had congregated from their different universities to London's Heathrow airport had taken about 7 hours, arriving at night-time to their hotel booked for the night. They left on the first flight out to Lagos the next morning, and after two days of cross-continental travel, couldn't wait to relax and get to accomplish the task they had planned and set for themselves over the past few weeks.

The hotel was small when compared to the standards of Boston, New York and London, and as they reached the end of the driveway, they saw a white man that they correctly assumed to be the proprietor of the hotel, along with several other men and women patiently waiting for them.

"My name is Joseph," the man said as they alighted from the vehicles, "Joseph Harold, owner of the Ikeja Arms Inn." This said as he extended his hand to shake of each of the five Americans guests to his beloved hotel.

"Ade, could you please show our guests to their rooms. I know it isn't much compared to the hotels that you've been in" Joseph said as he walked behind the men as their luggage was taken by the porters towards the rooms, "but I assure you this is the best in Lagos, and you will absolutely enjoy your stay here."

"We were told it was great, Joseph, right Bill?" David Henry said with a nod and look towards his friend and Amherst director of Admissions, Bill Wilson.

"Absolutely Dave" Bill replied, as he was being motioned towards his room.

"A colleague of ours was here a year ago advising on the proposed University of Nigeria in the east of the country that's being built. Spoke highly of your place, Joseph."

"Glad to hear that" Joseph said with a smile. "By the way, my friends call me Joe," stopping to leave his guests to the privacy of their room. "Dinner will be served by 6pm, just so you can get yourselves refreshed and have something to eat after your long journey here."

"Thanks Joe" David said throwing a one fingered salute from his temple.
"Glad to be here and looking forward to our weekend stay."

Joe and his staff thus left the American party to their own devices after ensuring that they had what they needed in their rooms and went back to the main building to await their arrival for the dinner service.

•

"It's been 34 years" Joe Harold thought as he sat in his favourite spot, under the huge Almond tree in the garden by the side of the hotel, enjoying the ever-welcoming evening breeze, as the enticing aroma of Jollof Rice and Chicken being prepared for the newly arrived guests in the nearby kitchen.

Joe had arrived in Nigeria in 1926, working first for Miller Brothers Trading Post and then for the Ministry of Supply in Lagos for the British government, before settling into the hotel business by sheer good fortune and happenstance in the mid-forties. First, he took over Grand Hotel with his late wife Beatrice, the societal hub for Lagos at the time, which every personality and politician frequented for the atmosphere, great food, and entertainment. It had been their great pride and honour to manage that great symbol of British imperialism in Colonial Nigeria, facilitators and observers to the interactions between cultures, English, Igbo, Yoruba, Hausa and many more.

Their experience at the running of that great place would be short-lived though, as the hotel would have to give way to more important development plans of the colonial government for the city, as the Nigerian economy grew.

Joe and Beatrice had already been bitten by the Hotel business bug, and in 1948 Joe bought a house in the remote areas of Ikeja with a dream to making it the "new Grand Hotel", which whilst lacking the prime real estate location of its predecessor, would eventually become a social hub in Lagos with the same kind of gusto and atmosphere that pulled so many people together.
He called this dream "The Ikeja Arms."

As Joe looked around the grounds in the gathering dusk, he smiled at the memories he could see; the mango tree he and Beatrice had inherited from the original piece of land housing the hotel, and which they preserved and worked around ever since they first tasted its fruit on the day they acquired the property; the flower arrangements across the grounds that Beatrice and the hired groundsmen had so painstakingly put together over the years, managing and sustaining them through the seasons, the Dry and the Rainy.

He could still see her now, walking among her favourite flowers approvingly, with a smile on her face checking for and pulling weeds, calling out to Ola the groundsman to bring some water and waving to him in the distance, even though 3 years had passed since her death…

"Joe!" He turned towards the sound of Jean's voice as she strolled across to him from the hotel entrance, so deep in his daydreams that he had failed to hear the car that had brought his wife home. They had been married about three years following the death of his first wife, Beatrice.

"You've been daydreaming again, haven't you?" Jean said as she reached him "Looks like it will be a lovely evening, and a great first night for our guests."

“Sorry love” Joe said, kissing her offered cheek. “Didn’t hear you pull up. How was your day at the hospital?”

Jean, who worked in the Colonial Nursing Service, was the matron at the hospital in Isheri, which while a relatively new hospital, was catering to the growing population of its environs, for as the business opportunities grew in Africa’s biggest city, so did its population which in turn meant more challenges for the city’s medical workforce, the precise reason why the hospital was built in the first place.

“Nothing too dramatic today so far by God’s Grace” She replied as they walked back towards the hotel. “The children from the car accident have been released. Thank God their injuries weren’t worse than they turned out to be. Their bones will heal quickly, having suffered only minor fractures as they are young, and as the flesh wounds are healing nicely. Car accidents are just something we are starting to see more of as the number of vehicles in the city continue to grow. Hopefully, the traffic service can get a handle of the situation and adapt quickly to better safety precautions for the populace.

Enough about me already. How are our guests?"

"They should be on their way to the dining room, any minute now" Joe said looking at his watch, as they paused to look around to see if their guests had come over early. "We have a treat for them" he continued "None of them have been to any part of West Africa before. We've got Jollof Rice and Goat meat being prepared."

"Can't wait to have some" Jean said as they got into their room. "Smells delicious. Told you the new cook Nneka came highly recommended."

"Absolutely agree." Joe said closing the door. "I was sad to see Fola go, and I'm sure she's happy to be closer to her husband, but those American lads are in good hands with Nneka's cooking and have a great weekend ahead of them."

•

Ade came to their doors at 6pm prompt, knocking on each to inform them that dinner was ready to be served, and then waited patiently in the garden just in front for the American guests to emerge. He didn't have to wait long.

David got out of his door first, followed by his Amherst counterpart, Bill Wilson, and they noticed Ade waiting in the garden.

"You're waiting to take us to the dining

quarters, right?" Bill asked.

"Yes sir" Ade answered, "Madam Jean asked me to tell you that food was ready and to show you the way to the dining room."

"Madam Jean?" David asked with a quizzical face "Who's that?"

"Ah" Ade exclaimed with a smile, "That is Mr Joe's wife. The nurse from the big hospital."

"Great" David smiled, "We are going to meet the lady of the house. Hey guys" He continued as he motioned towards the closed doors of his two remaining colleagues who were still indoors, "You ready yet?"

Their doors opened almost simultaneously as they were on their way out anyway.

Charles Doebbler IV, the Director of Admissions at Brown University, walked out towards the waiting party, then dallied as he noticed the other door open, choosing to wait for a colleague to catch up to him first.

He was a good man with a great future ahead of him with a passion to give the best opportunities he could to young people who wanted to pursue the rigours of University education, and especially African Americans, in the light of what was going on in the United States with the Civil Rights movement of the 50's.

The idea of helping young Africans fulfil their potential the same way as their American colleagues and coming to the Continent to ensure it was done right had proved too great a life-fulfilling experience to pass up.

"Hope we didn't keep you guys waiting too long?" Charles asked as he reached the waiting group. "We are starving and can't wait to taste whatever they've got for us. Smells great from here, right Richard?"

Richard W. Moll was another good man destined to do great things in the coming years in the American University system, and another one from the group of Admission Directors who had a passion to help students from the continent of Africa fulfil their potential. Representing Yale at the time, he too was in Nigeria for the very first time, looking to help steer the potential of the burgeoning countries youth to even greater heights.

He too had watched the Civil rights movement in the US fight for the basic rights of African Americans and did all he could to support them, not just because it was the right thing, and one which should not have taken all the killing and violence that had been a staple of that journey, but for reasons of his own as well.

As hard as it was for African- Americans to obtain the very rights promised to all in the Declaration of Independence, it was unthinkably difficult for the LGBTQ community at the time as well, and Richard was gay. As flamboyant as he's persona was, he still conformed with the societal norms of the time, especially as he was in a position of responsibility to young adults.

He suppressed a lot of his personality and watched the Civil Rights movement led by the notable figures of Martin Luther King and Malcolm X, supporting the cause where he could, and hoping for a day when he and the African- Americans marching in the street would one day enjoy the rights promised to all Americans regardless of sex, colour or creed. He wasn't sure when that day would come but believed it would happen in his lifetime and was determined that he would live his life as much as he could and wait to meet that day.

"Smells sensational, Charles" said Richard as they both reached the waiting group of David, Bill and Ade. "What's for dinner, my dear friend?" he asked Ade, who had started walking in a direction, prompting them to follow him.

"It's Jollof rice and goat meat, Sir" Ade replied with a smile, "You'll really like it very much. Just wait and see."

"I'll take your word for it" said David, as he and the others followed Ade through the corridors to the dining area, the aroma from the food getting stronger and more enticing by the second. "What do you think of the place guys, amid the little glimpse we've had of the country so far?"

“Looks great so far” replied Bill “Tell you what guys. Would have loved to stop and give those kids hawking the different products some money, even if it weren’t for what they were selling. Pretty brave of them to be doing that at their age. Hope they get to go to school too.”

“I’m sure we’ll get the opportunity to do that and more in the time that we have here” said Charles “The country is just brimming with potential.”

“I can’t wait to get started, guys” Richard chimed in. “Truly excited. But first, I could eat a horse right now. Whatever it is that’s been made for dinner, Jollof rice, was it? I can’t wait to get started on. The aroma is glorious.”

“Hey! There they are.”

Ade turned into a large room with tables with large, well-lit lamps hanging on the walls providing great lighting and surreal visuals like the Americans might have just stepped into a beautiful oil painting.
There was a long table running through the middle of the room to which they were being beckoned by Joe and a lady they assumed to be his wife, Jean.

"Come on in and have a seat, gentleman." Joe continued everything's ready and waiting for you. Please meet my wife and our great host, Jean. Jean, these are our American guests who've just arrived today."

"Nice to meet you ma'am. I'm David Henry, and the others are..." gesturing as the others on the team came forward to shake hands with Jean, "Bill Wilson, Charles Doebbler and Richard Moll."

"Great to meet all of you" Jean said after she had shaken hands with the team, "Please sit and have some food. Nneka, the hotel chef, has really put together a great feast this evening. Let's not hold you up any further, I know you've travelled a long way to get here. You need to get some rest tonight too."

"Thanks Jean" Richard said as he sat down." Great to meet you, and yes, the food looks great. Time to dig in guys."

"It has been a long journey ma'am" Charles said, tucking a napkin into his shirt as Jean directed a young lady named Dupe on serving the hotel guests. "A flight from New York to London, and then another one from there to Lagos. It's the longest journey I've ever undertaken."

“Do you all live in New York?” asked Jean as she surveyed the table, making sure that everything was in place as Dupe began serving the food to the Americans and her husband.

“No Jean” Bill answered, looking at the food being served and patiently waiting for all his fellow team members to be served. “We work for different American Universities, but we arranged to meet up in New York to make it easier to organise our trip, and also because that was the nearest International airport to all of us, from which we could catch a flight out to London.”

“How is old London” asked Joe.

“As great as she has always been” replied David, “I’ve travelled there once before, and she hasn’t changed much, that old great city.”

“We didn’t really have much time to explore the city” Richard added, but we intend to make the most of some layover time on our trip back to the States. By the way Joe, this is excellent.” He had just had his first spoonful of rice and goat meat stew. “Great stuff ma'am," he said nodding to Jean and the now departing Dupe.

"Thank you" Jean said, smiling. "I'll pass on your praise to Nneka.

"So, gentleman, what brings you to our neck of the woods." Joe asked, "And how did you find out about our humble place."

"That would be my friend Glen L Taggert who visited Nigeria last year, to help with the planning for new University in Nsukka, Eastern Nigeria." David said. "He stayed here initially before travelling to the east, and when he heard of our plans to visit Nigeria for our project, he recommended your hotel."

"As for our project here" He continued, "It's a new African initiative being organised by the United States to help fulfil the potential of the youth around the continent. We are still in the pilot phase now, which is why the team and I are here, to organise and actualise the potential of this new program into the life changing footprint we think it can have on the people of this emerging continent."

"Sounds great, David. Wish you guys, luck." Joe said. "There's a lot going on in the continent right now, I think it's only a matter of time before Nigeria joins a growing list of countries that will be granted independence from the colonial powers, Jean and I see it wherever we go, and I think it's the right time too."

"The country will need all the help it can get from the international community, and especially the youth in this country, they have so much great potential." Jean said." I see it whenever I go out into the community, which must do in my capacity as a Nurse. I'm glad the international community is taking an interest in the future of the African youth."

How are you planning on getting this done?" asked Joe, "It's a huge country with a large population."

"That's what we're here to figure out and organise with the help of the government here," said Charles. "Hopefully, we can get it all up and running in the not-too-distant future."

"Will you stay in Lagos for a while? Jean asked.
"Just for the next few days. Maybe a week" David said. We'll meet the Minister of

Education on Monday to get a plan and schedule together, and then we'll travel out to different parts of the country to start putting the framework of our plan together with regional coordination, to be able to reach across all areas of the country."

"That's great." Jean said smiling. "That means you'll get to enjoy a bit of the Lagos social scene. Trust me, you're in for a treat." And then, looking round at the table, she asked "How was the food?"

"I could eat that every day, ma'am" Richard said "It was sensational, and I'm not just saying that because I was hungry to start with, but I pride myself on my cooking and that, lady was top notch. Right guys?"

"Absolutely" Bill said "That was some welcome from you guys. I'm stuffed."

"Glad you liked it" Joe said, "And now I'm almost certain you gents will want to catch some sleep." This said with a glance at David whose eyes looked heavy and ready for much needed sleep.

David caught the look and smiled "We really do need our sleep but that was a tremendous meal tonight. Can't wait to find out what you guys have instore for us for the rest of our visit. And now if you will excuse us" He said looking round at the table and noting that everyone had finished their meal, then pushed back his chair and stood up "We'll be heading back to our rooms and will hopefully see you tomorrow morning."

"The pleasure has been ours" said Joe "Please follow Ade back to your rooms and let us know if there is anything you need."

"Thanks guys." Bill said as the group walked away "See you all tomorrow."

And with that, they followed Ade back towards their room, disappearing into the night.

•

David stepped out of his room, basking in the afternoon sunshine but wilting with the humidity even though his watch said it was 430 pm, when the temperature was supposed to be descending from its peak and heading down towards a supposed evening time cooldown. He tried to remember what the previous evening temperature had felt like as he strolled into the gardens surrounding the hotel annex where he as his colleagues were staying in and thought it wouldn't have been much different to what it was now. He had been told anyway that he would acclimatise to the temperature and humidity, the longer he stayed in the country.

He looked back at the doors of his colleagues' rooms to see if anyone was venturing out, but seeing no movement, he decided to explore the hotel grounds for himself.

The whole team had already been out earlier that day after Joe & Jean had acquiesced to Bill's wish to see more of the city and countryside for himself, and the others had come along as well.

Acting as a guide, the couple took the team on a ride through the fledgling city, showing them the spot where Joe's first hotel, The Grand Hotel, which had been the social hub of Lagos in its 1940's heyday, but had now been demolished and replaced by the national headquarters for Chase Bank and Pan-Am.

They went to the different local markets in the area, not necessarily because they needed anything, the Hotel staff had already done their weekly shop to replenish the

Hotel food and amenities, but just to get the Americans to experience what it felt like to buy and bargain for items in the market.

Obviously Joe and Jean had experience in the art of bargaining, and the visiting team of academics smiled and enjoyed the intricate back and forth between the sellers and their hosts, which would go on for minutes at a time before an agreement was struck that was acceptable to all sides, and then goods were passed across for the requisite financial compensation along with plenty of smiles from the Nigerian women and a few extra additions to the amount of stock they had agreed on, as a “thank you for your patronage” kind of deal.

Bill resorted to immediately trying his hand at his newly learned market bargaining skill, buying all sorts of knick-knacks and little edibles like groundnuts which immediately became his favourite snack from then on, exalting in this new experience.

The others followed his lead. Richard loved the design patterns on some of the clothing materials he saw at some stalls. The traders selling them called them “wrappers,” and after a period of negotiation he acquired a

couple for himself, to the delight of the woman he patronised.
Charles bought beads for his wife and, as the advocate of education for the under-privileged that he was, tried finding out using Joe's familiarity with the local language, if the children in the market all went to school on the days that they should, sighing sadly to himself whenever he encountered any child that inferred that they weren't.

They hadn't stayed too long, leaving after less than hour at the market as the afternoon temperature rose to its highest level after noon, with Joe and Jean fully aware that their American visitors weren't yet acclimatised to the humidity they would encounter in Nigeria.

Arriving back to the hotel shortly after 1pm, they then had lunch comprising of Pounded yam and Okro soup, one they thoroughly enjoyed, after which they each proceeded to their bedrooms to get some rest, having been told by Joe that there was going to be a party on the hotel grounds later that evening, with a lot of people coming for the "Night-time Dance" with the expected full moon providing a glorious lighting backdrop…

David had woken up earlier than the others, having never been much of a daytime sleeper himself, and so found himself wandering the hotel grounds.
He thought he could hear what seemed to him like radio commentary in the distance and decided to investigate for himself.

He happened upon a little group of people a short distance away, hurdled round what seemed to him like a radio, and one of them turned to towards him as he caught sight of David's movement from the corner of his eye.

"Good afternoon, Sir" he called out to David waving in his direction for him to come closer to them.

"Good afternoon to you too" David replied as he reached the group of Nigerian men and women "Nice to meet you. Sorry I don't know all your names" He had now noticed Ade and Dupe, who had now looked up as well as a few others he had noticed earlier.

"My name be Ola, Sir" the man who had motioned him over, announced. David in the local dialect of English, or as he had learned earlier that day, "Pidgin English."

"I be the groundsman for this hotel, and these people na the other people way dey work for this hotel like me."

He now stood up from his sitting position to introduce the other members of the group, one after another by name. There were Ade and Dupe, along with Segun who looked after the gate. Nneka, the lady he had heard so much about at the dinner table, the Hotel Cook as well as Bisi and Samuel, who looked after the hotel rooms and laundry.

David looked at him as he made the introductions. He seemed to command the respect of the group, and not just because he seemed like he was the oldest one, but something else he couldn't put his finger on. But as he started to get back to a sitting position, David noticed that he had a slight limp, and struggled for the briefest moment to sit down back on the ground.

"Are you okay?" David asked. "Do you have an injury of some sort."

"Ahh, don't worry Sir" Ola replied smiling. "It's an old war injury Sir. The pain comes and goes."
"An old war injury? Which war was that?"

"Ahh, the old war Sir. The Cameroun war" Ola answered.

David frowned slightly, not sure if it was polite to question the old man any further to find out what he meant, because he considered himself a student of history but had no idea which war was referred to as "the Cameroun War."

"He means the First World War, Sir" Ade interjected, noticing the look of confusion on David's face "He fought for the British as part of the West African force against the Germans in Cameroun, which was at that time colonised by Germany."

"Oh, I see now," said a relieved David. "That was a horrible war for everyone. You would have thought we would never have to fight another one twenty years later, but alas we did." Then addressing the old soldier, he continued.

"I'm sorry for your pain and thank you for your service. A lot of good men died fighting in that war. How did you get your injury?"
"We were charging toward enemy lines, Sir. The bullets hit me in my hands." He said, pointing at his arm (David smiled as he

realised that when he said, "his hands," he meant his arm) "...and in my leg" This, said while holding the thigh of the leg that David saw him favouring when he tried to sit back on the ground a while earlier. "Some part of the bullet is still there which is why I have pains, Sir."

There was a moment of silence among the assembled group following this last statement by Ola, which was then interrupted by the sound of static from the radio which snapped everyone's attention back towards the radio, and made David remember what had brought him towards the assembled group in the first place.

"What's happening?" He asked.

"It's the big game today" Ade answered as Ola fidgeted with the radio controls trying to locate a better signal." It's the game between Nigeria and Ghana in Lagos today. We have been listening to the game here."

"It's to qualify for the Olympics next year" Nneka said.
"It's always a big game when Nigeria plays against Ghana." Said Ade. "They have beaten us a few times already since we

started playing against them some years ago, but we hope to get them this time."

"The boys have been playing very well already" Said a beaming Ola "They make us proud. They are just small boys, very young. The match just started a small time ago, but already they are playing well."

"Mind if I just hang around for a bit and listen with you guys?" asked David as he moved a little closer and squatted next to the listening group.

"Sure Sir." Ade said, as he moved a bit to the side to help David get a better vantage spot to listen to the commentary.

"The goalkeeper Omiunu throws to the feet of Nnado, who lays it off to his defensive partner Okoye, who passes it to Achebe to avoid the pressure from the Ghanaian midfielder Gyamfi..."

"I can listen to that man for the whole day" remarked Dupe.

"Yes. Ishola Folorunsho is a great commentator" added Ola. He makes us feel like we are in the stadium watching with our own two eyes."

“He is among the first Nigerians to give commentary on our local football games” said Ade, turning towards David. “And he is just great. If we can’t make it to the King George V stadium in Lagos, we don’t feel like we are missing anything when he is commentating.”

“…Godwin Achebe and Anthony Onyeador combine beautifully to get away from the close marking of Odametey, giving the ball to the newcomer Christian Ohiri, who goes past two Ghanaians who looked like they were lost on the way over from Accra. He continues and slips a pass to Elkhanah Onyeali to avoid the attention of the Ghanaian central defender Oblitey, who passes it back to him. A gaping hole has appeared in the middle of the Ghanaian defence and Ohiri slips right through, looks towards the goalkeeper’s right and releases a thunderous shot to Baffoe’s left. GOOAAL! It is a GOOAAL. 1-0 to Nigeria!!!....”

The listening party jumped up in unison at the goal, shouting like they were in the stadium too. Even Ola, forgot that he had an old nagging injury and jumped up with everyone, wincing as he landed on his feet but smiling, nonetheless.

The scene reminded David of the touchdown celebrations he had been a part of during college football games, and he smiled as he watched them celebrate.

“That boy, Christian Ohiri, has been good” remarked Ola, as he rubbed his waist gingerly after settling back down to his earlier sitting position. “He plays like he has been playing for the national team for years even though he is very young.”

“He seems like he will be a great player for Nigeria in the future” remarked David, as he looked towards the house to see Joe emerge.

“Yes Sir. It looks that way” replied Ade. “We are gradually building a great national team, and soon we will catch up with Ghana.” He continued, beaming as he and the others settled back down to continue listening to the game.

“Well, I’ll let you guys enjoy your football game and I’ll go check on Joe over there. Best of luck with the results”
“Thank you, Sir,” Said Ola smiling “We will win.”

With that, David walked away from the excited group, who were back to being engrossed in the football commentary and made his way towards Joe…

•

David smiled at the memories from the Ikeja Arms hotel, as their vehicle slowed down as it made its way through a group of children hawking a few edibles along the road to Owerri, and Charles wondered out loud if they were doing this because they needed to raise money for school.

They were on their way to Owerri as part of their strategy to maximise their reach across the nation, as much of the country as they could. They had arrived in Enugu, the capital city of the Eastern Nigeria region just a week ago, and had already visited the city of Onitsha, the region's commercial hub.

The great education pioneer Alvan Ikoku was going to be in Owerri, and the American team had hoped to pick his brain on their strategy while they had been in Lagos but hadn't quite been able to meet him where he served as a Representative of the Eastern Region at the Legislative Council for the Colonial government there. When the news came to them that he would be visiting Owerri for a few days, not far from his hometown of Arochukwu, the American team decided to go down there to meet him, especially as they had also received an invitation to go from the principal of the great secondary school in the town, Government College Owerri.

But as their vehicle sped on towards Owerri, David was quietly more excited than he would normally be because the other thing he had learned while with the excited group listening to the Nigeria vs Ghana game, was that the great young talent they had raved about, Christian Ohiri, was also from Owerri, and he noticed that name on a list of young boys that the team of University Admissions directors, were going to meet…

CHAPTER THREE

Uchechi woke up to a cold November morning, the opening salvo from the fast-approaching Harmattan season, the second of Nigeria's two season weather pattern also known as the Dry Season, which ended the six/seven-month Rainy season. In addition to being the lesser humid part of the year in the country, it was also the weather pattern that brought the weather system from the Sahara Desert to the North of the country's borders.

It was the Saturday Morning of a weekend that had promised so much, making him wake up much earlier than he normally would on weekends. He went about his chores while most the household slept in the wee hours of the morning, progressing through them as quickly and as efficiently as he could. His first chore comprised of sweeping the front of the compound with the long broom made from Palm fronds. This, being the Harmattan period, meant that there were a lot of leaves to sweep up as the trees and plants all shed their leaves and a regular breeze blew them across the compound, but Uchechi hardly noticed the extent of the task ahead of him as he made short work of the leaves, sweeping them up into piles and then using the wheelbarrow to move the leaves to the designated point as directed by his father.

As he made his way back from his concluding wheelbarrow trip to dump leaves, he paused and stopped to listen and after a few moments started to make out the sounds of sweeping emanating from the next compound and smiled as he knew that could only mean that his friend Emeka, who also had the same area of responsibility in the Onuoha compound as Uchechi, had also woken up early in order to get through his chores, just as they had planned the previous evening before parting ways for the night.

The word had gone out during the week about a Sports try-out/audition that was taking place on the football field at the Government Secondary School, which was the Secondary School that Uchechi and Emeka went to. The news had come out of nowhere in the middle of the week, with an announcement by the school Principal, Mr Okoro, at the end of Morning Devotion on Wednesday. A murmur of excitement went through the students on Assembly ground, especially the big boys at one end of the crowd of assembled students on their final term of Secondary School.

As they headed back to their classes at the end of the devotion, Uchechi, Emeka, Chidi and the rest of their classmates talked excitedly among themselves about the upcoming sporting event, wondering why it was so hastily scheduled. Normally, sporting events were planned weeks or months in advance and so the boys speculated as to why this event had to take place with so little notice given.
Shortly after midday, Mr Okoro came to the Form 6 classes and called an informal meeting, with all the boys asked to gather in and around the classroom of 6A.

"Afternoon boys"

"Good afternoon, Sir," the boys of Form 6 replied.

Mr Okoro was a well-respected Igbo man in his fifties. He had become Principal 3 years earlier, a distinguished honour amongst the educators of his time, as Government College Owerri was widely recognised as being one of the premier secondary schools in Eastern Nigeria. He was liked by his students and almost as equally feared, with his well-earned reputation as being a disciplinarian.

He was also a family friend of Uchechi's family, being a distant relative of Uchechi's father. A few weeks earlier, Uchechi had confided to him about his desire to study abroad in the United States, when the principal had noticed him looking distracted and seemingly dejected whilst on one of his rounds to check on his students.
He had comforted the young boy smiling, as he explained to him the difficulties of financing such a venture and telling him that he too wanted to go abroad to study, having so admired the Christian missionaries that helped educate him all those years ago.
But then, just as it was now, such an endeavour could only be undertaken by the very wealthy, and not men of comparatively average means like Mr Okoro's father who was farmer, albeit a successful one.

"I know Henry, your father, will find it difficult to fund a university education for you abroad, even if he wanted to. But even more than that, I believe he is worried about the political climate in the United States with regards to Civil Rights. How your Uncle James has been able to thrive in such an environment, only God knows, but that uncle of yours has always been a strange one, come to think of it." This said with smile, as he seemed to reminisce on some memory or other. "But don't give up or lose faith, God makes all things possible, and we as mere mortals can never tell what plans he has in store for us." Mr Okoro was also a deeply religious man of Christian Faith and always emphasised the importance of the Christian Faith in the lives of his young students. "Put it in prayer, and never lose hope. If it is an endeavour that God has proscribed for you, He will find a way to make it happen."

Uchechi was replaying that conversation in his head, as Mr Okoro moved to the front of the class with two other teachers behind him.

"I hope you boys haven't been up to much mischief, eh?"

"No Sir." The boys all answered in unison.

"Good. I know you are almost finished with Secondary school now, with just a few weeks to the end of your time here, but I urge you not to forget to always stay ready. You never know what opportunities are around the corner, and we are living in a time when a lot of great things are happening in our country. We are seemingly on our way to independence from the British…."

"Ise!" the boys all chanted loudly, responding in the popular Igbo traditional affirmative response, drawing a smile from the adult trio standing before them.

"As I was saying" Mr Okoro continued, "A lot of things are changing all over our great continent and around the world, and it seems some of those changes are coming to our city of Owerri, courtesy of some Americans that will be visiting."

There was a murmur that arose from the midst of the boys as they started chatting to one another about the exciting news they had just heard, but wondering what the event was about. Uchechi's heart started to beat a little faster.

"Quiet" Mr Okoro bellowed towards the boys and was immediately rewarded with dead silence.

"That's better. Now, they have asked to talk to you when they come here to our school. They have said that they will come here on Saturday morning and will stay till the end of the day.

They will ask questions on your academics and will also like to see you perform in some sports events.
Yes Emeka?" He stopped, pointing at Uchechi's friend who had raised his hand.

"Sir" Emeka replied, stepping forward. "Did they say why they want to talk with us?"

"Apparently, they are the heads of Admission to some big Universities in the United States, and they want to see if they can find students from Nigeria that could qualify for scholarships to those Universities and Colleges."

The last bit of this sentence was said with a smile on his face, and quick look around the room as bedlam arose from the assembled boys, until his eyes caught the stunned look in Uchechi's face, which increased the smile on the face of the Principal, as a brief "I told you so" flashed across his face before the stern look returned, as the other two teachers present sought to quiet the boys down.
Once the students stopped talking, and a semblance of order returned to the meeting, Mr Okoro continued.

"You boys will not be the only ones present at this event. Boys from across this area will also be invited to join us here. We have been given the honour of hosting this event due to our school's place as the oldest and most prestigious in our area. So please, be at your best both behaviourally and academically. This is a unique opportunity that has become available to us out of nowhere. Don't waste it."

And with that he abruptly left the classroom with the other two teachers, leaving the excited shouting of the boys, and the open-mouthed look of surprise on Uchechi's face in his wake…

As Uchechi and his friends left school at the end of classes that Wednesday afternoon, walking through their school's back gate by way of the Teacher's quarters, they talked excitedly of the day's earlier news, speculating on which topics would come up for discussion when the Americans would interview them and also what sports they'd be asked to participate in.
"I hope we get to play some football" said Kachi, who was probably the best footballer of the group, with a good first touch and foot speed. He was the last born of the seven children his parents had and was a classic "last born" in the African family hierarchical sense, usually a lot more liberal in their view

of the world and laden with far less responsibilities than their elders.

"I'm sure you would" Emeka said smiling. He was Uchechi's best friend and like Uchechi, a first- born son, which ensured that they both had far more responsibilities in their household, with so much more expected of them from their families. Emeka's father was a prominent politician in the area who was well known and respected. He hadn't told the others yet, but his father had already discussed preliminary plans to send him to study abroad in the United States. He just didn't want to tell anyone until the plans were concluded.
"I'm more interested in the topics they'll be testing us on. Science? Arts? Current Affairs or politics, especially with what is going on across our continent?"

"Same here" echoed IK, who was the most academically gifted of the group. He was almost certain to gain a place at the new University of Nigeria being opened in Nsukka, a 3-4-hour drive to the north of Owerri, towards the northern borders of the Eastern Region of Nigeria. He had recently lost his father due to a sudden illness, which had caught the community by surprise, and had led to a period of grief for everyone who knew the family. Emeka's father, who was quite wealthy, had taken up helping with IK's school fees, which not only enabled IK to continue with his education, but brought the already close-knit group of friends even closer.

"I don't really mind either way" Uchechi opined. He was the best athlete of the group, average at football, which was the pre-eminent sport in Nigeria, but great at the sprint races, like the 100, 200 and 400 metres and was a solid student on the academic side of things.
His mind had been racing with the possibilities ever since the principal's announcement that afternoon. He had left the class quietly once Mr Okoro left to offer a quick prayer to God, being a strong Christian of Anglican extraction.
Ever since the "family intervention" had occurred at the family home about five months earlier, almost extinguishing the hopes and dreams he had of going to the United States to study in university, he kept praying for a miracle. The talk he had with Mr Okoro had helped to pull him out of his slump, along with some encouragement from his mother, both of whom told him to keep a positive mindset and trust in the power of prayer as well as a timely reminder

that great things come through for those who keep mentally strong in the face of adversity.

Still, Uchechi knew the odds were heavily against his dream of going to the United States but had decided to not think too much about the matter anymore, especially after conversations over time with his Dad Henry, who had also noticed the change in countenance of his son and tried to boost his spirits as best as he could, taking him along on trips to neighbouring towns like the great market city of Aba, second only in Eastern Nigeria to Onitsha.
Henry Chukwuka knew he couldn't afford to send Uchechi abroad, but he did not like to see the effect of losing that dream had on his first-born son and had quietly resolved to try all he could to see if there was another way to make that dream happen.

The shock that Uchechi felt, as Mr Okoro had informed he and his classmates, of the upcoming event, wasn't just that it had come out of the blue or the possibility of going abroad that had just presented itself, but that it was exactly an opportunity to the one country he had wanted to go to in the first place. As he had stepped out of the class to

pray, he had thought to himself "It can only be God."
The group of friends made their way through their schools back way and turned towards IK's house as it was the closest to the school and was a regular stopover whenever they left school together.

"Can I borrow the notebook we were talking about earlier, when we get to your house?" Asked Chidi, the only one in the group who hadn't spoken up about the exciting developments of the day.
He's Dad, just like Emeka's, was a rich businessman from a wealthy trading family in Aba, who had moved to Owerri to establish himself in a different market from the rest of the famous trading family. He wasn't really worried about going abroad, as his dad regularly travelled overseas on business and his elder brother was actually schooling in the United Kingdom.
"That way I can use it tonight, get what need from it and return it to you when we get into the class tomorrow morning before the lesson starts."

"That will be ok, Chidi" replied IK, "Just don't forget to bring it with you, tomorrow morning."

"Wow!" Uchechi exclaimed, "Isn't that Chris?"
Everyone looked up the road in the direction of Uchechi's pointing finger and strolling casually towards them was the one of the most famous men in Owerri, and the name on the lips of virtually every young person in the city. His recent football exploits were the subject of much discussion virtually everywhere you went.

His name was Chris Ohiri.

•

A former student of one of the rival Secondary schools in Owerri to Government College, Holy Ghost College Owerri, he had become celebrated due to his prowess on the football field and at Athletics events competitions both in the city of his birth, Owerri, and throughout the rest of the Eastern Region.

He had caused a lot of anxious moments for Uchechi and his schoolmates whenever the two schools clashed on the football pitch, and they were all glad when he graduated to attend Teacher Training College for two years.

But he's exploits had already caught the attention of perhaps the most famous footballer in the city, and in fact the country at the time, the great Dan Anyiam who would later have the biggest stadium in the city named after him posthumously.

So enamoured was he about Chris' football skill, that he pushed for him to be put into the national team that was to represent Nigeria in the Olympic Qualifying games for the forthcoming 1960 Olympic games in Rome.

The first game against rivals Ghana played in Lagos a few months earlier, had pulled most of the people of his hometown of Owerri to the nearest radio to listen to the play-by-play description of his exploits in the match. Dan Anyiam would not be playing, as he was above the Under-23 age group requirement for the football tournament, meaning all of Owerri's attention was centred largely on the young man making his international debut. His goal and superb play during the game lead to much celebration and talk in the town for a lot of the following days, as the town took pride in "gifting" to the budding nation, yet another football talent in the well-earned 3-1 victory.

The return leg in Accra carried with it, great expectations for the young upcoming star, his name on the lips of people throughout the city in anticipation of another great performance.
Maybe the weight of expectation was too much for the young star to bear, or maybe the Ghanaian team had gotten the tactics right having studied his game from the previous meeting.

Whatever the reason, Chris had a difficult game that day to the disappointment of the Nigerian football fans at large, but sympathy from his hometown folk. The 4-1 loss to the bitter rivals Ghana and subsequent failure to qualify for the coming Olympics lead to criticism of the team, and as the newest member of the team, whom some saw as being parachuted into the team due to the perceived influence of his mentor, Dan Anyiam, he became the target of much of that criticism, forgetting his great play from the previous game and his young age.

He had returned after that game to the town and carried on with his life as it was before all the hoopla, putting finishing touches to his teacher training course and continuing his preparation for his athletic events that he

would represent Nigeria in, for the Olympics in Rome.
That was a representation of how much talent Chris had. Even in the disappointment of his football outing for the country, so vast was his talent that he was going to still represent Nigeria in another sports endeavour.

Uchechi had greatly admired the talented prodigy for a couple of years now, even though he had represented a rival school then, as he was impressed by not only Chris' athletic ability, but also by the way he carried himself and the respect that everyone who knew him, had for him.
They had developed a mutual respect and friendship over the last year, as they had mutual intellectual interests, with both being a few of the many young admirers of the Pan- African movement that was pushing for Nigerian independence from Great Britain lead by the great Nnamdi Azikiwe, Obafemi Awolowo, Sir Mbonu Ojike, Akanu Ibiam and Michael Okpara amongst others. They had met at a few NCNC political youth rallies, the party being the dominant in South-East Nigeria, and with Igbo people, basking in the political tide of popularity and pride, that the independence was riding on.

“Kedu” said Chris, the Igbo word for “How are you?” as he approached Uchechi hand outstretched with a smile on his face. “It’s been a while. I hope you’ve been keeping up with your Athletics training?”

“Not as much as I should have” Confessed Uchechi, as he pulled his hand away from Chris’ grip to their mutual amusement, with Uchechi thinking to himself that it had indeed been a while since they last met, as he had forgotten Chris’ playfully strong handshakes.

“You need to keep pushing to improve your times, brother” Chris said as he moved to shake the hands of the other guys, as he knew them all in various degrees of familiarity, as was the case with people growing up in the small city of Owerri. “It’s the only way you can get to that elite level we spoke about before. Seems like you guys are done for today. Anything exciting happening?”

“Surely you know about the visit by the Americans?” asked Emeka. “We’ve been told that people from outside our school will be coming.”

“Yes, I heard. The news got to me yesterday while I was training.” Chris said. I saw one of them briefly as he moved around the training ground with some of the city sports officials. I’m going to be there this weekend.”

“You’re going to be there too, Chris?” Uchechi asked.

Chris smiled as he looked round at the group in front of him, and at Uchechi in particular. “Everyone that is eligible to go for higher learning based in and around Owerri, will be there. This is a once in a lifetime opportunity, totally unexpected. We just don’t have enough Universities in Nigeria to cater to the needs of our country. You know I wanted to go to university myself but had to go to a Teacher Training College instead.”

“I didn’t think of that” Onyekachi said. “The principal said people from outside our school will attend the program, but if what you say is correct, we can expect a lot of boys to attend.”

That exact thought was what had prompted Uchechi to ask the question concerning Chris’ attendance. The talk concerning the sports trials had given him some hope as to his prospects for meeting whatever performance criteria that would be required, as he was fairly confident in his athletic prowess.

With the understanding now that there would be a lot more boys coming to the event, and therefore a lot more talent present, talent that he had never gone against or measured himself with, with no greater talent than his great friend Chris.
The hopeful feeling, he had only a few hours earlier, didn't feel as genuine a vibe as he had felt earlier. A lot more work and preparation would have to go into this than he had previously thought...

Chris seemed to read Uchechi's thoughts accurately, and maybe a few of the others as well. "There're quite a few places up for grabs according to the little information that I heard. If you perform to the level, I know you're capable of," This bit said directly to Uchechi, "I'm sure you'll scale through whatever athletic standards they are looking for, never mind the academic ones which I'm sure you guys are ready for regardless."

"Thanks for the vote of confidence, Chairman" said Emeka smiling, and the whole group burst into laughter, with any rising tension and anxiety that started to hover in the air dissipating as quickly as it had come.

“So where are guys headed” Chris asked.

“Well, first we’ll stop over at my house” IK replied, “After that, I’m not sure what everyone is doing. I’ve got some house chores to take care of this afternoon.”

“How about you Chris?” Uchechi asked. “Where are you heading to?”

“I’m going to check on my friend Dozie on the other side of your school. I haven’t seen him since I came back from the match in Ghana.” He paused and quickly looked round at the group for any facial expressions depicting negative feelings about the ill-fated match and saw none.

“We are so proud of you, brother.” Uchechi said, “I knew you were great, but nothing prepared us for what we heard out of our radios concerning your football skills. I wish I were present there to watch it for myself.” Chris smiled as the others came forward to shake his hand, echoing similar opinions. He bade them farewell, and they went their respective ways.

*

It was 7am Saturday morning when, Uchechi and Emeka made their way towards their school. The birds sang ceaselessly in the trees that lined the road and, occasionally, a sound of rustling emerged from the bushes and plants which made up, along with the tress, the forests that surrounded their neighborhood.

Their neighborhood was situated along the valley of the Nwaorie river that ran through the town of Owerri. From his home at one part of that valley, Uchechi could make out the walls of Holy Ghost College, the rival secondary, towards the top of the hills rising from the valley of the river.
It was always a sight to behold whenever he stepped outside of the family home, especially at that time of the morning when the fresh cool breeze that seemed to emanate from the river, swept through the air, softly caressing everything in its path.

They walked along the road through the neighborhood, greeting the few people they passed, moving quickly as they had discussed the prior evening. Uchechi had

wanted to get to the school athletics field early to loosen up and get some practice runs in.
The schedule for the program had been revealed to the boys on Friday morning after the morning assembly, increasing the excitement among the boys as the day of the assessment grew closer. Ever since their encounter with Chris a couple of days earlier, Uchechi, his friends and the rest of the Form Six students had been running afterschool practice sessions in a few sports; athletics, football and Wrestling; trying to make sure they were razor sharp for the weekend trials.

Within the school hours, they also arranged lessons amongst themselves in various subjects like English language, Mathematics, Physics and Chemistry amongst others, trying to anticipate the areas in which the Americans would pull questions from, whilst improving any shortcomings they might have in any of those subjects. It wasn't much a laborious process, as the boys had just finished with the A Level exam and they were all still relatively sharp, intellectually speaking.

The duo stopped over at IK house where they found him waiting for their arrival, from where they then proceeded via the back entrance to the school, as it was closest from IK's place. They said their greetings to the few teachers they passed, as they made their way through the teachers' quarters on the way to the school field just right round the corner.

The schedule had revealed the start of the program as beginning at 9am that morning, so Uchechi and his friends had agreed to meet at the field at 7am and get a jump on the other people who would be coming for the program. That way, they could get some work in for an hour maximum, and then head to the classroom for some final revisions of the subjects they had been studying for since news had broken of the opportunity.

But as the trio of boys turned the corner, to their surprise, they came upon a crowd of boys in the field. Not just their schoolmates, but also boys that they didn't recognize, who must have come from the surrounding areas and schools as Mr. Okoro and Chris had intimated to them a few days earlier.
Quite a few people it seemed, had the same idea that Uchechi and his friends did.

There were a few people doing sprints, while most others just stretched and spoke to one another. Nigeria was in the middle of the harmattan season which basically eliminated much of the humidity and making the temperature much cooler that it usually would be. That, combined with the early morning time, made it more feasible to try any physical activity. Everyone was aware that there were going to be interviews conducted by the visiting American university administrators that would test their academic abilities, and no one wanted to be sweaty or dirty to attend those interviews, and based on their various observations of white men, didn't think any of those interviews would be held anywhere near the open field, not with their averseness to the heat conditions in Nigeria that they weren't used to.

After walking around for about half an hour, Uchechi and his friends, the rest of whom had now joined them on the field, decided that they would head back towards the classroom to try and get themselves prepared for what they assumed would be interview sessions with the Americans.

As they approached the classrooms, they saw Mr. Okoro heading towards them in the company of a few teachers, as well as some White men that they assumed to be the visiting American university administrators. Two of the teachers veered towards the field that the boys had just come from while the rest of the party continued towards the Assembly Hall, which was the building where major school events and ceremonies were held.

Uchechi's heart rate spiked as he and his friends entered their classrooms, the same feeling he usually had whenever he was about to write an exam, as they all knew now with the sight of their Principal and the Americans, that the interview/selection process was about to begin.

They quickly got into a huddle in the classroom and began their revisions of the various subjects that they taught they might need. They took turns questioning each other on various topics for about an hour until the senior Physical Education teacher for the school, Mr. Chukwumerije, came to the classrooms around 830 am to summon Uchechi and his friends, along with the rest of their schoolmates who had all now returned from the field, or arrived from their homes to the Assembly Hall for the event that was to start in thirty minutes.

It seemed like all the boys of Uchechi's age from Owerri and its surrounding areas, had arrived at the Government College Assembly Hall for the event. As they approached the hall, Uchechi and his friends kept running into friends that they knew either from church or other some other means outside of the school. They kept exchanging pleasantries with anyone they knew, forgetting for a moment the event that had brought them all together that day.

"Alright young men" Mr. Okoro's voice boomed from the doors leading to the hall, "There are too many of you to fit into the hall. So, what we are going to do is get several of you in at any one time. By God's Grace, we have good weather today. We'll arrange you outside in groups and then we will get each group to come through these back doors, and after you finish your interview, you will exit from the front door. Does everyone understand the plan?"

"Yes Sir". The candidates gathered outside the building answered.

"Good. Let's begin now. Some teachers will start to arrange you into groups of 50. Please do not scatter the groups after the

arrangement has been made. Hopefully, we will get through this process quickly and then move onto the next phase, which will involve some physical activities."
"Sir". Someone from the crowd asked, "What kind of physical activities are we going to participate in?"

"The games earmarked will be some Football and Athletics. Nothing else. Just think of it as a bit of fun and relax. That alright?"

The boy answered in the affirmative, upon which three teachers began the process of arranging the boys into groups, so that the interviews could begin.
Uchechi and his friends quickly observed the process and then arranged themselves into a position that would enable them stay together in any proposed group, to which they were eventually successful.

Uchechi then looked around at the gathered boys and noticed there were a few girls present. Once they were noticed by the teachers, they were put together in the first group and sent into the Assembly Hall for their interview.
Amongst that first group Uchechi observed, was his friend and the most popular person

present, Chris. He caught Uchechi's eye as he entered the hall and waved. Uchechi waved back thinking that it was only right that the person who had brought much pride to the town should be given the first shot at the interviews.

The groups outside watched as the boys and girls began emerging from their interviews and then going off to one side, as they had been instructed not to mix with any groups who had not done their interviews.

Soon enough it was the turn of Uchechi's group, and they tentatively made their way through the double doors at the back of the hall and into the benches that had been arranged for them to sit on. As they sat down, they noticed the four Americans seated on the stage along with Mr. Okoro and a few teachers.

"Morning young men" Mr. Okoro greeted the boys, rising from his seat after all the prospects had been seated. "Welcome to this part of the selection process for this great, new opportunity that has been afforded us by the great American institutions that these men seated here with me, represent. I'll allow them to introduce themselves." He sat down and one of the Americans stood up to address the group of young men seated before them.

"Good morning, guys. My name is David Henry from the famous Harvard University in Boston, Massachusetts and seated with me are Bill Wilson from Amherst College, Richard W Moll from Yale University and Charles Doebbler from Brown University." Each man stood up with a smile and a cheerful "Hi" to the assembled young men, as their names were mentioned.

"We are all from some of the greatest institutions of higher learning in the United States". David continued, clearly acting as the spokesman for the Americans. (Uchechi and the others would later learn that the Americans had taken turns in addressing each of the other groups).

"We too were once a young country as your country is now, getting our independence from Great Britain, just as Nigeria is about to in a short while if things continue to progress in the direction that they are heading now. But no country can fulfill its potential if it doesn't have a pathway for its youth to be educated to unearth the potential, they have in themselves as well.

Right guys?" To which the others nodded in the affirmative.

"With that understanding, the schools we represent along with both the United States and Nigerian governments, have decided to come up with this scheme to get some of you over to the United States to study as there is currently only one University in Nigeria, which will not be enough to cater for the demand for places for the young people to study. We wish you the best of luck for this. Our enquires won't be complicated, we just want to know more about each one of you, just to help put us in a better position to make the best decisions with our selections. Thank you, and once again, good luck."

With that, they began calling up each boy, starting from the benches closest to the stage from left to right, to approach the stage and provide names to identify themselves.

From Uchechi's position a little further away from the stage, he and his friends listened to the enquires made of each applicant on various topics ranging from Government, Geography, history and of course English amongst others. They quietly smiled at each other in self-congratulations in their ability to have maneuvered themselves to such a prime position where they weren't the first to be interviewed, giving them an advantage in having prior knowledge of what to expect.

The questions didn't seem difficult but did seem random based on the conversations that progressed during each interview, so by the time it got to Uchechi's turn (he was the first from amongst his group of friends), he felt confident about whatever line of questions the Americans would decide to pursue.

"Morning young man" Bill asked him as he approached the stage, "What's your name?"

"My name is Uchechi Chukwuka, Sir."

"What does your first name mean?" Richard asked pleasantly "We are aware that your names mean something in your language, and it's been great learning the meanings of the different names."

"Uchechi means the will of God".

"That's a great name" Charles said, "Maybe that's a good omen for this exercise, wouldn't you say?"

“God is always with me, Sir. I know and trust in that” Uchechi said smiling.

“That’s a great belief system, you have.” David said “tell me, what do you know and think of the United States? What have you heard and what things apart from schooling would you like to do if you go there?”

Uchechi took a deep breath, looked up at the four Americans seated on the stage in front of him, and at Mr. Okoro who was watching the whole exchange closely, and then back into the gaze of the visitors.

“I want to travel to America to study and observe all the things that I’ve heard about that great country. The people, cities and cultures. I want to see all the things I’ve heard about from my uncle of your country. Of course, the main reason I want to go there is to become an engineer, so I can build great things like Mr. Henry Ford, but my parents have always taught me to observe your environment whenever you go to somewhere new, so you can see how things are done and learn things that you can use to increase your knowledge.
My father said sometimes you don’t know that there are better or other solutions to

doing things until you observe someone else do it and learn."
"My country" Uchechi continued, "is a new, young country, and I want to go out into the world and see how things are done so I can bring that knowledge back here and help improve and grow my country,"

There was silence from the Americans on stage and a smile from Mr. Okoro, as Uchechi finished his impromptu speech, and little nods of agreement from the visiting school administrators.

"That's a great take on life, Uchechi" Richard commented. "I can see you have great parents" he said smiling. "They must be proud of the man they are raising."

"That was a great answer Uchechi" Bill added. "Your thoughts encapsulate what we envision for the African students coming over the United States."

After that, there were just a few questions that seemed more routine than anything else, as it seemed they'd gotten the answers that they wanted from him, and after which he was asked to use the side door to leave the hall, just as others had done previously, but he felt a strong sense of satisfaction and confidence in his prospects.

He stepped out of the side doors just as the other prospects had done earlier. The rest of those prospects were now standing around on the Cricket pitch, which was next to the hall and at the center of the school property. Others were hanging around the nearby classrooms or anywhere that provided a sitting opportunity or a chance of shade from the emerging sun. He looked around for familiar faces, greeting them and sharing thoughts on the interview experience they had just passed through. After a while, he spotted Chris, surrounded by a group of fellow applicants and obviously sharing stories of his exploits with the National team just a few weeks before, judging by the way everyone in the area was paying rapt attention to what he was talking about.

A few of his friends began stepping out of the hall as well, having completed their interviews. They waited until all the group had exited the hall, and then they moved towards the area where Chris was and joined the throng of people around him. Sure enough, he was talking about the football games he played against Ghana, and especially about his impressions of the West

African country that was the first country on the continent of Africa to achieve independence, only a couple of years in 1957.
Chris noticed Uchechi and his friends come over to the edges of the crowd surrounding him, and slowly made his way towards them.

"What did you think of the assessment?" He asked the group, once he got close to them.

"It was ok, actually" Emeka said. "The Americans came across as nice people too. The whole experience was a lot better than I thought it would be."

"My thoughts exactly" Chris agreed. "There were a few questions concerning the courses we would want to pursue over there in America, but for the most part I think they were more interested in our character as individuals."

"True" Uchechi said, joining in. "I've never met an American, and whilst some things I've heard from my uncle about them don't show some of them in a great light, I thought to myself as they asked questions, that these men were a great group of guys."

"I wonder what they have instore for us later on, during the games event." Wondered IK.

"Same here" Chidi agreed. "It will be very interesting to say the least, especially with the crowd gathered here today."

They all then looked around the school, as their contemporaries milled around, talking, laughing and huddling together around anywhere they could find to sit down and wait for the next round of this potentially life changing day.

"Should we head towards the field now?" asked Uchechi. "We were the last group to go into the hall, and from what I can see they will soon be done with the interviews as almost everyone is now outside the hall with us."

"That sounds like a good idea" Chris said. "I don't know about you, but I'm getting a little bored just standing around waiting. Let's see what we can do, or what's happening out there on the field."

With that, they made their way through the classroom areas that bordered the field and made their way to the expansive school football pitch. There were already quite a few people already there talking among themselves and seemingly preparing to run some sprints or something of that nature.

"I wonder which athletic events they are likely to get us to participate in" Uchechi asked. "Anyone hear anything about any potential games or events we'll be participating in?"

"I believe we were informed that there would only be football and athletics" Chris answered. "And I did see some of your teachers with a few footballs earlier on. New ones too. I won't be surprised if we had a game of football or two, with the sport being the most popular sport not just in Nigeria, but in the whole continent of Africa."

"I agree. Chidi said. "It looks like we have some good athletes present today, though."

They had just witnessed a 100m sprint race comprising of about 7 guys, and from the pace of the race from start to finish, it was easy to tell that the runners were fast athletes.

"I know those boys from athletic competitions across the Eastern Region." Chris said. "They are some of the best athletes in our region and are also looking to represent Nigeria in the upcoming Olympics in Rome, next year. Didn't know they would be coming here also for this, but this is also a great opportunity for them as well."

Uchechi took a look around at the people now streaming into the field, and it dawned on him that not only was he going to have to bring out the best of his athletic abilities, but he was also going to have to compete against some of the best in the entire Eastern Region, some of whom spent a lot more time than he did, pushing themselves in competition, a fact reinforced again at that very moment, as a second group took flight on another 100m dash.

Everyone now seemed to be on the field, as the interview stage of the day had now concluded, with the Americans and the School Principal along with some of his teachers, making their way from the Assembly Hall to the school field.

"Alright everybody, gather around." Mr. Okoro said once he and his guests had reached the field. "This is what's going to happen in the next hour or two. We are going to arrange some games for you to participate in. There will only be two events that will take place. 100 meters races and a football match. You can only participate in two 100 meters race at a maximum. We don't want anyone to be overly exerted, we just want to have a look at your abilities, as it will potentially help your American school know which non-academic activities, you'll be alright to participate in, to help better integrate in your new surroundings, should you be among those chosen to go."

"We will check your race times to see who was best at the sprints. After that, we will have a game of football, where you'll have the chance to show off those skills of yours, for those of you who have them, that is.". That brought laughter out of the assembled group of boys and girls.
"Also, as we don't have as many girls here today, you ladies will have just one 100 meters race to run, which we will observe in the same way as the boys.
Goodluck everyone, the School Games Master, Mr. Nnado, will now get you all organized for the events."

With that, everyone was put into Groups as the Americans, and Mr. Okoro and the other teachers took strategic positions around the field to observe the proceedings.

There was much laughing and playing around as the 100m sprints began, with great cheering around the field as the races progressed.

Uchechi was the only one of his friends to make it to the final races. Chris was a given due respect for his undeniable athletic exploits for the country, and was asked not to participate in the races, but to take part in the football game that was to take place a little later, more for the viewing pleasure of everyone present, especially the American visitors, than anything else.

But as Uchechi had rightly observed earlier, he could not best the really gifted athletes that had come around for the occasion. The stopwatches merely confirmed the fear he had the first time he had seen the others race on his school field.

Downcast, he slowly made his way to the edge of the field to be by himself for a little while to gather his thoughts as the races concluded and arrangements started for the football match to come.
He backed himself on his intellectual performance from the earlier interviews, but he had really wanted to shine in the game's bits too, just so he could have an even better

chance of being selected for the chance of a lifetime that he had dreamed about months before the Americans showed up in his town. Emeka and the rest of his friends came over to cheer him up, just as he had done for them when they too had failed to progress to the final stages of the games.

Chris watched his friend as he walked off the field. Uchechi had intimated him on his dream of going abroad months earlier, and he had thought of Uchechi when the news first broke about the visit of the Americans to offer scholarships. Chris wasn't too surprised that Uchechi hadn't made the final stages of the games and was not sure if his friend had created enough of a strong impression to make the grade of the America's selection criteria for the scholarship.

"Alright" Mr. Nnado called out. "Everyone should come back towards the field. Let's get ourselves into a few teams and play some football. We will play only for about 15 minutes at a time so we can give everyone who wants to play a chance to play. That should be enough for us to judge your abilities. Good luck boys"!

Chris made his way towards Uchechi as Mr. Nnado began putting the boys into teams and spoke to him quietly. “Stay close Uche. Let’s see if you’ll get selected to play with me.”

“Alright”. Uchechi said a little confused pleasantly surprised. “I’ll stay close.” He had played a few games with Chris, but never in a competitive sense. More for fun than anything else.

They were indeed picked together, with Chris asking Uchechi to play wide on the right, while Chris played his preferred central attacking role. Chris, in addition to being a great individual player with great skill, was also a great teammate who knew the inclinations and skillset of each player and how to bring out the best in them for the good of the team.

He remembered Uchechi’s game well and was determined to help him showcase it in front of the Americans as best he could. Uchechi was tentative at first, but with encouragement from Chris, along with a few well-placed passes his way to the excitement of the crowd, he came alive and grew confident enough to display a few skills himself, drawing applause from the spectators.

“That boy looks good” David said turning his head in the direction of Mr. Okoro.

“Which boy?” Mr. Okoro asked squinting at the field.

“The boy playing Outside Right on Chris’ team. Who is he? He can play, but I don’t remember him being on any sports teams.

“Ah. You must be talking about Uchechi.” Mr. Okoro replied smiling. “I believe he was also one of the boys that impressed you during the interviews.”

“Well, well. What do you know! Looks like he’ll be a great prospect for one of our schools. Please help me make a note of his name.”

“Absolutely. Will be my pleasure. He’s a good boy…”

The team won by two goals to one in an entertaining affair, much to excitement of Uchechi and his friends and even the star of the show, Chris.

After a few more matches, Mr. Nnado the Games Master announced that they had concluded with the assessment, whereupon Mr. Okoro asked everyone to go home and wait for an announcement on Monday, after a consultation with the visiting Admissions officers.

Tired but excited, the candidates left for their various homes exchanging stories as they walked home.

Uchechi and his friends took their usual route after exchanging goodbyes with Chris. Uchechi pulled aside Chris for a moment.

“Thank you for helping me through this. You have always been a great to me, but this one I won’t forget. God Bless you.”

“Anything for a brother” Chris replied smiling, and after shaking hands with the group, turned and melted away into the distance.

CHAPTER FOUR

Uchechi looked around his bedroom like one would do if they were entering it for the very first time. The big cardboard box in the corner where he packed away virtually every textbook and exercise book he had used since his primary school days.

Another corner housed the chest of drawers in which he kept his clothes, both the ones he currently wore and the ones that he had grown past, that hadn't been picked up by his younger brothers. Those drawers now lay largely empty as most of the wearable clothes in them had now been transferred into the suitcase that lay on the ground next to it.

He looked at his younger brother's empty bed, free momentarily from the ever-enquiring human menace he shared the room with. He smiled as he thought to himself that he would have sworn only a few weeks ago, that the thought of not seeing his brother for any stretch of time would have been a very welcome development. But as he heard Nnamdi's voice emanating from the living room, a strange sadness came across him and he wiped a tear from his eye hurriedly.

He checked around the rest of the room thoroughly one last time, just to make sure there was nothing he had missed and just as he could confidently confirm that he wasn't leaving anything behind, his father's voice sounded from the doorway to his room.

"Are you sure you have everything? You're not leaving anything you'll need behind?" Henry Chukwuka asked.

"No Papa. I have everything packed away into the suitcase now."

"That's good my son because the car taking you to Lagos is here. You are going to need to get used to the fact that you need to prepare yourself in advance from now on. You will not have me or your mum to rely on as you might have in the past. You are a man to the world. An independent, capable man, just as we discussed yesterday. Never forget, my son. Never forget."

"Yes Papa. I'll be fine, I promise. You have always taught me well, Papa."

Henry Chukwuka turned quickly to exit the room, and without turning his head spoke in a low voice. "Have you checked with your mother to see if she has anything else for you?"

"She asked me to come to your room after I finished packing."

"Alright. Make sure you do that now, before we start getting your things into the car".

With that, he left as quietly as he had come in, without a look back, but with a distinctly sad demeanor about him, shoulders slightly slumped as if he had suddenly acquired the weight of the world on them.

Uchechi followed him out of the room but turned in the opposite direction as he made his way towards his parent's bedroom, where his mum told him that she would be waiting in…

The past few weeks had been a whirlwind of activity, ever since he had found out that he had been chosen, as a part of the inaugural group of West African students to study in the United States on scholarship, after a nerve wracking few months of waiting for news.

Mr. Okoro himself had driven down to the house to speak to Uchechi's parents, who both exploded into great cheers and clapping that attracted the attention of the neighbors, including Uchechi himself who was in Emeka's house playing a game of football with a few other friends.

The hoopla brought him running back into his house with his friends trailing behind, and running into the scene of his father calling out to anyone present to bring out the fresh palm wine for his friend and his mum rushing off to prepare something for him as well, but not before noticing Uchechi's entrance and grabbing him in a bearhug and excitedly telling him that Mr. Okoro had just informed them that he had been chosen to go to America.

For the first few weeks after that, there had been somewhat of a carnival atmosphere in the Chukwuka household. Travel plans were immediately put together. Enquires were then made to the government officials organizing the venture as to what things were needed by Uchechi, documents and other things, that would be needed to make the trip, and report successfully at the school.

Uchechi had also been informed that he had been chosen to attend Harvard, which brought even more pride to his parents, as they knew the prestige of the great University. Even more to Uchechi's liking, he discovered that his great friend Chris Ohiri had also been chosen to go that same great bastion of education in Massachusetts.

But as time drew closer to the time of departure for the United States by Uchechi and his fellow successful applicants, it also began to dawn on the family that for the first time in their lives, one of them would no longer be physically present in the house. Not just for days or weeks, but potentially for years.

That knowledge quietly started to make it to the fore of family discussions and conversations. Uchechi noticed a gradual sadness from his mother whenever she saw him, and longer, more frequent conversations with his father ranging across several subjects.

Akunna Chukwuka insisted on taking her son to the markets to walk with him as he bought some of the things he was going to need for the coming intercontinental sojourn. They would have long talks about all kinds of things on those trips, a lot more than had been the case as those trips were usually reserved for his sister Ngozi.

At first the trips irritated Uchechi, for even though he loved his mother very much, he didn't quite see the point of all those trips and some of the conversations, but after a while he began to understand what she was really doing and started looking forward to those talks, as he began to realize as time for his departure drew closer that he was going to miss her too.

His father also made time to take Uchechi to the palm plantation and his other work interests. They would spend time talking about the pros and cons of the various projects, but conversations eventually would migrate to the need for discipline and responsibility in one's life and work to be successful at anything they did. Also, the importance of respect for others, pre-planning and dedication to the tasks at hand would come up amongst others, and just like Uchechi had begun to understand with his mother, he grew to appreciate even more than he had previously, what his father was doing.

His friends also started to come around to the house even more than they usually would. They had all basked in the excitement of Uchechi being one of the few from the entire Eastern Region of Nigeria to make the list. In fact, virtually all his former schoolmates had come down to the house at least once from their various homes, some coming a longer way than others.

They had all now completed their Secondary school education and were on the way to their chosen paths of adulthood and life. Some like IK and Onyekachi were going on to the new University further north in the region at Nsukka, that was to open its doors in October that year. Others were going on to Teacher Training Colleges to become the next generation of teachers and educators, while others were going off to learn a trade or join family members in a business.

But just as Uchechi had noticed with his family as the time for departure was confirmed and drew close, an air of sadness seemed to occasionally burst through the atmosphere when he and his friends sat together as they all realized that they might not see each other again, or at least not for a long time, a totally new experience for a group of friends that had known each other and been together for most of their lives.

Further developments had come to light for the group, when news came round that

Emeka was also going to be attending Columbia University while Chidi was going to study in the United Kingdom. One way or another, the entire group of friends were all going to be leaving the town they had come to love and spent all their lives, some further away than others, but all far away regardless, to places they had never been before, with neither friend nor family present.

The day before Uchechi and Emeka had sat together under the tree at their favorite hideaway spot not too far away from their neighborhood. It was their final meeting as they contemplated Uchechi's impending departure for Lagos the next morning, on his way to catch a flight to New York, enroute to Boston and eventually Cambridge, Massachusetts the hometown of Harvard University.

"Have you packed everything properly?" Emeka asked as they basked in the golden glow of the evening shade, with the humidity trending towards its depths of the day.

"I think I've been packing for two whole weeks" Uchechi replied, to which they both broke out laughing, easing the solemness of the occasion as they had been in silence for virtually all the way there from Emeka's place.

"My mother takes me out with her almost every chance she gets, as does Papa, and I am reminded daily to check and make sure I've gotten the things I will need together. But I understand now. This is the first time that I will be leaving, and we have no family friends in Massachusetts. I know they are worried about me just as much as they are proud, but I can't wait to go and see everything. How about you? When are you travelling out to New York?

"I think I've flying over there about two weeks after you get to Boston." answered Emeka, "My Dad has a friend who lives in New York, and I will be staying with them at first until I know more about the city and am comfortable moving around. I think the plan will be for more to stay in the University residence halls by my second year. What's the plan for you, as in where you'll be living? Will you move into the residence halls straight away?"

"No. From the information we've gotten from the people in charge, I will be placed with an American in Boston and journey into Cambridge each day for lectures for I think maybe the first year or so, until I have become acclimated to and settle in, and then I will be then move to the University Hall of residence. It feels like a dream sometimes still."

"Do you feel afraid sometimes too? Emeka asked "We'll be going to a country where we everyone we know is far away, with a different culture and we'll be gone for a long time."

"Yes Emeka, I feel that fear sometimes, which is weird to me because only a year ago I prayed to God to grant me the opportunity to travel to America, but now that it's here, I feel both trepidation for the future and indescribable joy at the same time. On one hand, I can't wait to get on an airplane for the first time in my life and journey to the land of my dreams, and then at other times I look at my mother, father and siblings and wonder when I will see them again. Just the same way I wonder when we will gather under this tree again or catch up with the rest of the gang."

"Don't worry brother, we will all meet up again. Under this very tree, one day soon." Emeka stretched his hand out towards his childhood friend smiling "Shall we shake on it?"

"Yes brother" Uchechi replied, laughing as he clasped the hand of his childhood friend in their traditional handshake "We will meet here again someday soon. They better not think of cutting down this tree by the time we get back, or someone will hear from me!"

Laughing hard now at the thought, they stood up to make their way back home, as Uchechi's parents had implored him to get back home earlier as it was his last night before travelling.

"Hey Uchechi" Emeka suddenly said as they made their way home in the gathering darkness, "How are we going to keep in contact when we both travel over there? My father said the distance between the two cities isn't a lot by either train or bus, but we are going to have to figure out how we will find out exactly where the other person is in a country we've never been to."

"I think I'll be able to write letters to your school addressed to you, but even if that doesn't work at first, my parents will know how to contact me through the letters I'll write them and will be able to pass on that information to your family, and I'll be able to get your contact information through your family in the same way."

"That makes sense. Once we do that, then we'll be able to communicate better and even meet up! Imagine that" Emeka said excitedly "The two of us travelling on trains!"

Excited as to the future possibilities, the two lifelong friends walked briskly home, the forlorn air of uncertainty that clouded their earlier walk, now forgotten with the promise of a magical tomorrow…

•

"You're ready to go" Uchechi's mum asked as he came into her room. He looked around her room and spotted her huge suitcase open. It looked like she had been rummaging through it. He saw his childhood photo album lying on her bed open as well as some other photos of the family from across the years strewn beside it. He looked up at his mum and noticed her sad face. It looked like she had been crying. He felt himself resisting a strong surge to do the same suddenly.

"Yes mama. I have everything packed and ready to go, and the car taking me to the Motor Park is here now."

"That's good. Now sit down with me for a bit, let me talk to you." She said motioning him to sit on the edge of the bed beside her. "I want you to remember everything that your father and I have talked to you about concerning your travel abroad. Remember all the values that we have thought you; honesty, punctuality, hard work and finishing whatever you start.
I don't want you to just go over there and jump around from place, enjoying America. This is a great opportunity that has come your way which a lot of people desired to have, but by the Grace of God you have been chosen for it.
Don't waste it, do the very best you can so that you won't have any regrets later.
I didn't say that you shouldn't enjoy yourself. I just don't want you to spend so much time trying to enjoy yourself that you forget the goal of being there in the first place.
This is the first time you will be going abroad. It's a great opportunity to learn how other people who look different from us do things. Some things I'm sure you'll like and others, you will learn to stay away from. But

be observant so you can learn quickly. The quicker you learn, the easier and faster it will be for you to adapt to this new way of life.
I'll be praying for you always, both your father and I, and God will be with you always, and most important of all, don't forget to write us every chance you get. I'll be waiting for that first letter, we all will, so don't forget…

With that, she stood up and pulled her first son into an embrace, for which Uchechi was glad, as he had just at that moment lost his battle to keep his tears from suddenly showing.

The held on for a about a minute, and then she moved away and asked him to follow him to the kitchen where she had prepared something for him to eat on the long journey from Owerri to Lagos.

The rest of the following ten minutes was a bit of a blur in his mind as the family began helping him put his luggage in the car, as they realized that the time for the bus to move from the motor park was speedily approaching.
Emeka and his parents had also come over to watch him go, and the picture of the entire

group of friends and family waving to him as the car pulled into the road towards the motor park, was a memory that would remain seared in his mind for years to come…

•

The motor park was bustling with people and movement at that early hour of the morning. Uchechi's parents had made the arrangement for him to catch the 7am bus heading out of the park enroute to Lagos from the Ojukwu Transport Company. It was owned by the first Nigerian millionaire, Sir Louis Ojukwu, who was also from the Eastern Region and Igbo.

He was the first visionary businessman to see the need for transport across the entire country, starting in the northern region of the country in aftermath of the 2nd World War. He began with the transporting of groundnuts, grown in the north, to all commercial centers of the British colony before diversifying to other commodities and of course, the commercial travel industry.

Being the original transport company and trusted brand, he was the go-to person when important travel plans were hatched, and so on this most important day for the Chukwuka family, they were the ones entrusted with taking their son to Lagos enroute to his first sojourn outside the country.

His luggage was put in the back of the bus and after checking to see where it had been put, he went in and sat at one of the available window seats in the middle of the bus just as he had been instructed to look for by his parents.
"It's always the safest bit of any transport vehicle" his father had cautioned.

He had arrived and settled in with twenty minutes to spare, and so he and the rest of the passengers who had arrived early, waited for the 7am departure time to reach. In the meantime, there were food vendors milling around the park and the individual buses, looking for anyone who might need some food, fruit or snack for the journey ahead of them.
There were sellers of rice, roasted yam, fruits such as Bananas as well as those selling groundnuts, cashew nuts and biscuits.

Uchechi politely declined the offers to buy food, smiling as he clutched the wrapped plastic container that his mum had given him which had a meal of Jollof rice and plantain inside. He had never been one to eat on a journey, but he had never been on such a long journey before, one of about eight to nine hours as he had been informed, and so kept his food on his person. He also had light nylon bag filled with groundnuts, a favorite snack of his father, who had given it to him along with a few last-minute instructions for his trip.

The bus left on schedule at 7am without an empty seat on board to the delight of the ticket office and began its journey to the first of its stops in Onitsha, the biggest trade market town in all West Africa. They sped along the road past Awo-mmamma, Mgbidi and Orlu before getting to Ihiala.

He noticed the Igbo dialect of the roadside food vendors begin to change around Orlu to an easier listening version, a dialect he had rarely heard in his hometown, and even then, only from a person or two who came into his orbit on occasion. He had forgotten how nice it sounded and was the first time he had heard more than a few people speak it. By the time they had stopped at Ihiala to allow

someone on the bus a toilet break, the air positively buzzed with it. It was a big market town and was the first time on the trip that he felt he was on the outside of his home, even if in a pleasant way.
The break was brief, and they were soon on their way towards Onitsha, and they there in about an hour.

Uchechi had been to Aba, the second biggest market town in Eastern Nigeria with his father and he had been impressed by the sheer size of the market, which sold virtually everything a person might need. But once the bus rolled past the famous Upper Iweka part of Onitsha, Uchechi's mouth hung open at the sight of the biggest market he had ever seen.

It wasn't just the size of the market, but also the gigantic structures that housed quite a bit of the market, or at least the parts that he could see for it stretched far into the countryside from what he could make out as the bus drove along the road.
His father had once told him of the sheer size and opulence of that famous market, but even that reverential tale didn't do justice to the sight before him. Rows upon rows of market stalls, large and small, selling literally everything under the sun.

The dialect he had heard at the Ihiala stop came at him in a crescendo of sound. He knew people came here from the entire sub-continent, but they obviously adapted to the people of the town because that was the only language he heard. He had never actually realized how much he loved hearing the dialect, and so he immersed himself in the sounds of the great city as they drove through it. The number of food vendors and sellers of other things had quadrupled from the number they had encountered at Ihiala, and he was tempted to pick up something there, just to say to himself that he had bought something from the great city, but remembered he was on a strict budget and thought better of it as he remembered why he was on the trip in the first place.

As the bus crawled through suddenly visible traffic, Uchechi caught sight of what was going to be the highlight of his trip. His parents had excitedly told him to look forward to it, but they could scarcely have managed to convey the magnificent sight that laid before his eyes.

The river Niger was the longest river in West Africa, and the 3rd longest in the entire continent behind the Congo and White Nile rivers, respectively. It flowed through most of West Africa and into the Atlantic Ocean, basically splitting Nigeria in half coming through the North. Onitsha was built on its bank, as a lot of great cities tend to be, and the town of Asaba lay on the other side of the great river.

Uchechi couldn't see the bank on the other of the river as it was so magnificently wide. He now realized why there was traffic, as he saw they were waiting for the Asaba-Onitsha ferry to take them across the river, so they could continue their journey.

Once it got to their turn and they drove onto the ferry taking them across, everyone stepped off the bus and admired the river from the railings of the ferry. It was the most beautiful thing that Uchechi had seen and one he would never forget. As the journey had progressed, he had struck up a conversation with the man seated across from him, who was headed to Lagos to take up a new job, and together they had marveled at the great gift of nature from God, trying to look at the length of the river stretching in each direction in the distance, as well as the fish in the water below.

Once across the great river, they continued their journey to Lagos, going through Benin and Ore. The former was site of the one of the last great old West African empires whose incredible artwork had been looted and scattered across the world after the ancient city was sacked in 1897 by British forces. They stopped here so that passengers could get something to eat if they wanted to and use the restrooms available at the stop.

The latter town Ore was the town where they began to discern the speaking of the Yoruba language, the dominant language of the Western region of Nigeria. It was also the last major stop before Lagos, and where Uchechi finally succumbed to eating the meal that his mum had prepared for him, as he was so hungry. He didn't understand much of the language apart from a few words his parents had taught him but saw that the people were very amicable.

By the time they got to Lagos, Nigeria's capital and the largest city in Africa around 6pm, Uchechi couldn't wait to get off the bus. His travel weariness was somewhat assuaged by the sights and sounds of the great city. Even then, he could detect that the pace of life there was quicker than it was back home.

His newly acquired travel partner helped him find the local bus headed to the area where he was going to stay in, with a family of old friends of his parents.

They bid each other farewell, knowing they would likely never meet again but appreciative of each other's company on such a monumental trip for them. Wishing each other good luck on their respective pursuits, they got in their respective buses and headed off into the gathering darkness…

CHAPTER FIVE

The arrival time at Logan airport in Boston was 7pm, after a marathon flight that took Uchechi and another beneficiary of the American scholarship initiative who also was to attend Harvard University, from Lagos onto a New York bound flight, where he met up with Kofi, a recipient from Ghana.

Officials from both Nigeria and Ghana had put respective students on planes from Lagos and Accra respectively, having coordinated with Harvard University on how the boys would be picked up once their flights arrived at New York's LaGuardia airport.

Uchechi's flight landed first, whereupon he met Matt, the man from Harvard's admission school who was waiting for his arrival, as per the arrangement with the two West African education ministries via telephone earlier in the week as well as the previous day.
After introductions and greetings, they sat down to wait for Kofi's flight which was expected in an hour.

His first ever flight experience had been surreal for Uchechi. The whole process from checking-in his luggage, passport control to being ushered in with the rest of the passengers to his flight, and then when onboard being greeted and shown his seat by the beautiful red haired air hostess.

He had been on a high ever since he left Owerri, experiencing one new adventure after another. This time, as he laid back in his seat feeling the vibration of the aircraft engines, he almost couldn't stop himself from punching the air in delight, but he remembered his father's teachings about decorum in public spaces and kept his cool.

The announcement from the flight captain brought a smile to his face as he peered out at the tarmac from his window seat at the airport workers moving the last bit of luggage into the plane's cargo hold. The sound from the engine started to increase now, giving Uchechi an insight as to the power of the engines that lay in the aircraft.

As the plane started to taxi forward, Uchechi excitedly peeked out of the window after following the flight crew's instructions about his seatbelt, trying to make out what

he was looking at as the plane moved at a steady speed down the runway.
The plane then rolled to a stop after making a turn onto what looked like a long part of the runway, bringing a look of confusion to Uchechi's face. Within a few seconds the engine sound increased dramatically building up to a steady, powerful hum before he felt the g-forces push him back into his seat as the plane moved forward, catapulting itself across the runway before slowly lifting off to Uchechi's delight with buildings and structures gradually growing smaller by the second as they made their way through the glorious morning sky.

The flight had gone on without incident, apart from his panic when he realized that he was going to need the bathroom. He hadn't wanted to eat anything but realized he was hungry once the flight crew started distributing refreshments to their passengers. He had held out for as long as he could, until he was able to get the attention of the red-haired lady who had welcomed him onto the plane, and she smiled understandingly as she led him down the aisle to the bathroom.

The rest of the flight he spent looking through the window, marveling at the technology that had made it possible for man to take flight and travel across the world. The sensation of flying through the clouds, and at other times over them, felt like being as physically close to God as one might feel. And while he had marveled at the width of the river Niger on his way to Lagos, it was nothing compared to the unending expanse of the Atlantic Ocean.

He slept after a while until he was woken by the captain's announcement that they were about to land. That part of the flight was the only bit that had given him an anxious feeling. The plane felt like it was dropping away from him at times as it descended towards New York, suddenly and sharply dropping by what seemed like a few feet a few times, until he was able to see the city begin to get visible with each passing minute. Uchechi only got comfortable after the plane had touched the runway at LaGuardia.

He hadn't minded the wait for Kofi, as it gave him a chance to look around at the world-famous airport along with its unending movement of people and goods. It was the first time he had seen that many white people in one place, and the first place in America that he had stepped foot on, an event that would merely have passed as a dream a while ago.

"Do you want to get anything to eat?" Matt asked to which Uchechi replied in the negative, so engrossed in his observations that he had barely heard the question.

Kofi's flight landed shortly after, and Matt went off to bring him over to where Uchechi sat, as their Boston flight was only an hour away from taking off.

The introductions were brief when they returned, as they then made their way to the departure gate for their Boston bound flight, but Uchechi felt somewhat relieved to have another African face for company, and they quickly struck up a conversation as they moved to go through the flight departure protocol.

Kofi, another one of the fortunate 24 that had been chosen to be a part of this great scholarship scheme, had grown up in Accra, the capital city of Ghana where he was leaving his family with bated breath awaiting news of his safe arrival in the US.

The flight to Logan Airport in Boston was short and uneventful, with Uchechi already feeling like a veteran of air travel after his marathon flight schedule and wanting to get to his destination.

Both he and Kofi took their luggage as they followed Matt towards the exit, walking past a line of yellow-colored taxis patiently waiting for passengers to take into Boston. They walked through the various pedestrian crossings to the area where Matt had parked his car. With their luggage safely ensconced in the back they proceeded to drive through Boston, as Matt explained the final stage of their journey that day.

“Alright Uchechi, you’re up first. We’ll be driving to the Boston street address where you’re to stay for this summer, as you get used to the way things run here in the United States. The Clarkes are a good family, and we know they’re going to take care of you. Kofi is going to another address, as both of you couldn’t stay with the Clarke family, but your address is closer, so were heading there first.”

The Americans had thought it wise that their new African students spend the first summer in the United States with some preselected families which would help that adjust to conducting their lives in a completely foreign environment. The thought process was that the quicker they adjusted and felt comfortable with their new surroundings and people, the easier it would be for them to adjust to their educational objectives.

Uchechi looked around him in awe as they drove through the city. The beautifully lit streets, the perfectly finished roads, the endless stream of cars going in the opposite direction, in almost perfect formation. And then, as far as the eye could see in every direction, all types of buildings; skyscrapers, hotels adorned with giant neon signs and others.

But as they came off the main roads into narrower looking streets, Uchechi realized that they had come into what looked like purely residential areas, but which didn't look like the ones he was used to back home. They all looked the same and in perfect distance from one another. A few had American flags hanging from their porches. There were only a few people on the street, some huddling together under what looked like a sign, as if they were waiting for something.

As promised by Matt, the journey to the home of the Clarkes didn't take long, and they must have been waiting for his arrival because no sooner did the vehicle stop, did a middle-aged lady open the front door and walk outside towards the street with a man just slightly behind her in tow.

“Good evening, Matt” She said as she reached their parked car, smiling. “Glad you made it, and right on your estimated arrival time, too. I hope the journey went without a hitch?”

“The journey was great Catherine.” Matt replied as he got to the back of the car along with Uchechi and Kofi to help the boys get Uchechi’s luggage out from the car boot. “And you’re right. We made it in good time. How are you doing Clifford? The last sentence was spoken to the man following behind Catherine.

“Doing great Matt.” He replied, “Now let’s get you boys inside.”

“Oh, we can’t stay. I’ve got to get Kofi to Melrose, where he will be staying this summer.” Then, motioning to Uchechi, he introduced them to the couple.

“Uchechi, this is Catherine and Clifford Clarke who you’ll be staying with over the summer. Catherine, Clifford, this is Uchechi, the student you've been told about all the way from Nigeria."

"Well, Uchechi, I pronounced it right?" Catherine asked.

"Yes, you did" Uchechi replied, with a small smile, as she hadn't really pronounced it right but had been close enough, and he instinctively thought it was going to be something they'll get right with some help from him, with time. Besides, his father had told him about White people having difficulty pronouncing African and other foreign names, a lot of the time until they were either corrected or had gotten used to them.

"Alright then" she continued smiling back," Let's get you inside and settled. And what's your name?" She asked Kofi to which he answered.

"Hopefully, we'll get to meet again, but I guess you must be tired from the long flight to get here, so I'll let you and Matt get to Melrose to meet the family you'll be staying with."

"Welcome to America by the way" Clifford said to the departing duo as they got into the car to begin their journey to the Massachusetts city. "Safe journey, guys"

"Thanks, you two." Matt replied "I've had some time getting to know Uchechi and he's a great kid. I think you guys are all going to get on well. Goodnight."

With that, he started the car and drove off down the street and into the fading light, with Kofi waving goodbye to his newly discovered friend.

Uchechi waved back until the car was out of sight, and for the first time since he had left home, felt a sadness, for it was the first time since that fateful morning in the driveway of his parents' home, that the enormity of his journey hit him. All through the journey here to the front of the Clarke's home, there had been something or someone familiar that hadn't made the journey seems as far from home as it had been.

The road trip to Lagos had been with fellow travelers of mainly Igbo origin, and even when he had passed through areas that weren't of his tribe, they hadn't been strange, as he had met someone from there or had heard the language before.

When he had stayed in Lagos, it had been with people that his family knew and trusted, as well as people that spoke his language. And still, on the flight to the United States there had been other Nigerians that he had said a word to or two, as they were all united in the knowledge that they were all going to be foreigners, living in or visiting in a foreign land.

Meeting Matt at the airport, hadn't changed much in the perception of his surroundings, maybe because it had been just that, an airport, with thousands of people milling around, coming from and going to various destinations, just as he had. Meeting Kofi had brought an air of familiarity to his surroundings. A fellow African, on a quest like the one he had embarked on. A meeting of a potential new friend at school, one that would have a similar background to him, a luxury he knew would be in scarce supply in the coming years.

Watching Kofi drive away with Matt, felt like a goodbye to anything he thought familiar, and as he walked towards his new, temporary home with the Clarkes, he felt alone and far from home for the very first time.

Catherine seemed to sense the slight change in disposition from her young visitor and spoke to him once they had gotten inside. “You must be tired, and I don’t know what you’ve had to eat all day as you’ve travelled, but we have some dinner for you, once you’re ready and if you would like some.”

“Thank you, Catherine,” Uchechi replied. “I’ll have some if that’s okay.”

“That’s settled then” Clifford said, “Let me show you your room so we can get your stuff in while Cathy gets the dinner together.”

Uchechi looked at his hosts for the first time, in the lighting in the house. Catherine was a beautiful and graceful looking lady in her mid-forties, with a kind face and eyes that seemed to almost always be happily amused, and Clifford was an older, taller slightly balding man, who had a jovial nature to him when he wasn’t seemingly studying every situation with a serious look in his eyes, as if he were deciphering morse code. Uchechi would later get to learn that not only was he very intelligent, but he was slightly short-sighted.

They both walked towards the more interior part of the house, to a room roughly half the size of the one Uchechi had grown up in back at his parents' house. He smiled at the sight of a bed and noticed the wardrobe in the corner, which was different and superior to the one he had shared with his younger brother back home.

"We'll let you settle in and then we'll see you at the dining table in a bit." Catherine said, for she had followed them to make sure Uchechi was settled in properly. "I made you some macaroni and cheese. Don't think you've had it before, but I can assure you it's great."

"And very American" Clifford added, smiling, "A great way to settle in."

"Absolutely" Catherine added. "Alright, we'll let you be now, until we see you for dinner."

Uchechi looked around the room after his host couple had left, opened his luggage and took out his toothbrush and a few other things he thought he'd need right away, and then smiled as he made his way out of the room towards his promised dinner. It had taken over a year, but here he was, he'd made it. He was in America.

•

Uchechi walked down the street, the backpack that Clifford had taken him to get the previous day, slung over his shoulder. It had taken him a few weeks to get acclimatized to the American weather, even as to his amusement Catherine had told him that this season, summer, was the warmest time of the year.

He was wearing a pair of blue jeans and long-sleeved red shirt underneath his jacket to keep himself warm in the early morning August temperatures. Everything he wore, right down to his shoes, were brand new, befitting a student going to Harvard University for the first time, and being a foreigner, he didn't want to stand out in a wrong way, as he had learned from his Uncle James that Americans had a retrogressive view of the African continent and its occupants, no thanks to the images broadcast and stories reported by the media here.

"Don't be surprised to get questions about life, living in the bush or up in trees." James had laughed as he narrated some of his experiences, "But make sure to correct that impression every chance you get, whenever such a question comes up. But even more importantly, they will watch you and observe the way in which you conduct yourself, both academically and socially. In the end, the best rebuttal you will have to counter those perceptions will be your conduct and what you do, which I can assure from experience they'll be observing as they don't get to see many of us Africans over there."

Uchechi also remembered the cautions from his parents about conducting himself in a foreign land, and making sure that he kept his name clean, and to make a great first, as well as overall, impressions. As far as they were concerned, he was not just going over there to give a good account of himself but was going there to represent the whole Chukwuma family as well.

It was 7am as he strolled down the street, but there were already quite a few people moving around, on foot, getting into their parked cars, and then others walking towards what he now recognized as bus stops, and he turned on the sidewalk to notice one of the buses coming down the street to pick up the group of people that were patiently waiting at the stop.

He loved riding the bus on the occasions where he needed them to get to some places in Boston on his own, especially in the early weeks of his arrival when he was getting to know the city and would procure a ticket to enable him to ride the buses to his heart's content.

But today, he would be getting the train from Andrew Station to Harvard University in Cambridge. It was the first day of registration for new students at the esteemed institution. It was only his second time going there by train, as he had done a practice run the week before, just to make sure he knew which train to catch and how long it would take to get there.

As he reached the intersection where Boston Street met Dorchester Avenue and Southampton Street, which was always busy as everywhere seemed to come alive with people headed in all directions, both to and from the station, which was nestled in the corner just after the intersection.

There were young people like him that he assumed were headed for a school of some kind or the other. Some dashed across the street to catch the public buses approaching the stops for their time slot. Some younger ones were accompanied by parents towards bright yellow buses clearly marked for school that also had their pick-up points.

Uchechi walked into the street level area of the station along with a steady stream of other commuters, and then proceeded to go underground via the long flight of steps, an experience he relished just as he had done the very first time that he had used them, the very first experience in life that he had of walking deep into the ground and earth.

He made a mental note to tell his parents about it the next time he called home. He waited in line to pay for his travel, a tinge of excitement running down his spine as he heard the mechanized roar of the trains going through the station just a bit further below.

After he was done with Fare Control, he made his way to the platform to catch the train headed to Harvard University in Cambridge, happy that he had made the decision to reconnoiter his route as he was sure footed about what train direction he was meant to be on.

The next train came shortly after he got on the platform, and he followed the steadily growing number of commuters onto the train and sat down on the nearest available seat. He was the only Black man on the train.

He had experienced something new when he had gone into to town a couple of weeks earlier, but he had been prepared for it, both by advice from his Dad, and a small conversation with Clifford when he had first asked for directions in order to go out to buy a few things for the impending school year, and to get a measure of the city of Boston.

"Just be careful when you go into the stores today son." Clifford had said in a quiet voice. "You're a stranger in town, and sometimes… not everyone reacts the way they should to people they don't know or the type of people they don't get to meet often. Meeting you will be a new experience to a few people you'll see, especially with you having come from Nigeria. So, just keep calm if you run into…circumstances like that…"

“Don’t you think it might be a good idea to go out with him this time.” Catherine asked, with a hint of worry her voice after Uchechi headed towards his room to prepare, and she thought he was out of earshot.

“We’ve done that a few days ago.” Clifford replied. “He’s going to be going off to the University soon anyway, and its best that he gets used to moving around comfortably on his own…”

Uchechi had heard the exchange and knew exactly what Clifford had been trying to subtly tell him because his father and Uncle had made sure to let him know the problems of racism that lurked in American society.

Whilst Clifford had uncomfortably danced around the topic as best as he could, his dad and Uncle had painted a stark picture of the ways in which he had to navigate the racial problems he would certainly face.

“I wish it didn’t exist my son, and it is an ugly reality that you will have to face sometimes, but I will have failed in my duty to you as a father, if I didn’t make sure you were prepared for those experiences.” Henry Chukwuka had told his first-born son.

Uchechi had noticed the eyes that had followed his every move in the stores he went to, the frosty replies to some of his enquires from the payment counters compared to the friendly interactions to the white customers ahead of him on the line. He had heard a few monkey-like sounds on the streets when he walked along the sidewalk, and that on the bus coming back home, that no one appeared to want to sit on the seat opposite him.

So, when he got on the train headed to Cambridge, he first made sure to get a seat that was in the corner and not with anyone beside it. Rush hour was still a while away, as he would come to learn, and so he sat in peace to enjoy the ride to his new school.

The stations came by one after another; Broadway, South Station, Downtown Crossing and Park Street, each time passengers got on and off, but he noticed that most of the ones getting on were of a younger age now and thought that they were likely students just like himself, headed to Harvard.

The next station as announced was Charles Street, and as they pulled out of the station, they burst out of the monotonous underground setting of the journey into the brightness of daylight, with the skyline of downtown Boston suddenly on full display in all its glory.

They were now on a bridge crossing, with vehicles running almost parallel to the train, a short distance away, but even more spectacular was the view of the Charles River, the beautiful river alongside which the great city of Boston was built.

Uchechi could make out a flotilla of boats and yachts moored to the shoreline below and dreamed of one day getting on one of them and sailing away down the shoreline to better appreciate the beauty of the view.

Soon enough, they went back underground, passing through the final few stations along the Red Line, including a stop were a lot of young people that he thought were students disembarked from the train at the Kendall stop, which he later learned was the stop that serviced the famous Massachusetts Institute of Technology.

Then finally came Harvard, and everyone stood up to leave the train as the doors opened and began the walk up the flight of stairs headed to that bastion of first impressions, the Harvard Yard.

He had been here once before on the reconnaissance trip, but he hadn't really ventured into the school as he instinctively wanted to leave that experience for the first time he would need to go into the hallowed University. But as the crowd of young people around him surged up the station steps into the street, he just followed the mass of bodies through a small walkthrough entrance that most of the crowd he was around, seemed to favor.

Now however, he was confused as to where to go next. Every building in the yard looked like a church or palace from the great civilizations gone by, and each one had streams of people emanating from it.

The architectural design of each building held Uchechi in awestruck wonder. He had imagined that the University would be something special, with all the tales he had heard about its place in the history of American education, but even all that veneration of this bastion of achievement still fell short of the actuality that he could see right before his eyes, Uchechi thought. One building rose into the sky with a spire atop it and another, the one that gave off the feel of being the residence to some great king or ruler, had stairs that matched the impressive width of the building's front.

He strolled towards the building with an expansive flight of stairs leading up to its entrance, deciding that it would be his first port of call with regards to pointing him in the proper direction to begin the process of his registration.

While on his way to begin his march up the stairs, his eye caught a plaque with an inscription which read.

BY THE GENERAL COVRT OF MASSACHVSETTS BAY
28 OCTOBER 1636 AGREED TO GIVE 400 £
TOWARDS A SCHOALE OR COLLEDGE WHEAROF 200 £
TO BEE PAID THE NEXT YEARE & 200 £
WHEN THE WORKE IS FINISHED & THE NEXT COVRT
TO APPOINT WHEARE & W^T^ BVILDING
15 NOVEMBER 1637. THE COLLEDG IS ORDERED
TO BEE AT NEWETOWNE

2 MAY 1638. IT IS ORDERED THAT NEWETOWNE
SHALL HENCEFORWARD BE CALLED CAMBRIGE
13 MARCH 1638-9. IT IS ORDERED THAT THE COLLEDGE
AGREED VPON FORMERLY TO BEE BVILT AT CAMBRIDG
SHALLBE CALLED HARVARD COLLEDGE.

Uchechi read the inscription again, getting more disappointed by the minute. He wouldn't boast about his proficiency in English, at least not there, but he was certain something was very wrong with the grammar, spellings and a lot more in such a publicly displayed plaque.

He didn't know any German but was certain that whoever had done the inscription didn't either and had picked a bad time to experiment a desire to write in two languages within the same document.

Disappointed and uneasy, he began to make his way up the steps to make enquires concerning his registration and maybe get an explanation on the thinking behind the plaque he had just read.

He was halfway up the steps when he heard his name being called in the distance.

“Uchechi...Uchechi!”
He turned and striding towards him with a joyous smile on his face was his great friend, Chris Ohiri.

•

Chris Ohiri had of course also been selected as a recipient of the scholarship as Uchechi had been, but due to his commitment to the Nigerian team for the 1960 Olympic games held in Rome, he arrived the United States a little later than his fellow recipients.

Whilst he had fallen out of favor in the Nigerian football team due to the painful exit from the qualifiers, his incredible talent also warranted inclusion in the Athletic team representing Africa’s most populous colony and soon to be most populous country.
Due to those commitments, he hadn’t travelled to the United States around the same time when most his fellow scholarship recipients were doing so.

Uchechi had kept track of his exploits at the Games, trusting in the drive and preparation of his famous friend and living his Olympic dream of breasting the tape as a winner through the enigmatic Owerri man.

There had been much fanfare in the land when another Igbo son became the first Nigerian to win in an international sports event during the 1954 Commonwealth Games held in Vancouver, Canada. Emmanuel Ifeajuna was celebrated across the nation for his gold medal in the High Jump event at those Games, with everyone taking pride in that individual achievement, with it being the first time a Nigerian was recognized internationally and proved that we could excel in those spheres of excellence too.

Chris had not been successful at the Games, but Uchechi couldn't wait for him to get back from Rome so he could find out about what life was like at the Games village for athletes.

Whilst they had spoken before Chris had departed for Lagos enroute to Rome, they hadn't been able to exchange contact details to meet up in America because nothing had been finalized concerning their lodgings or time of travel at the time.

The hope was that they would somehow meet up with each other once they were both ensconced in the school, so when Uchechi saw the 6-foot frame of his friend bound up the steps to meet him, it was like he had been transported back to the familiar surroundings of his hometown, Owerri.

“When did you arrive brother?” Uchechi asked as they clasped hands and then grabbed each other in a bear hug, drawing looks from the throng of students milling around the yard.

“Just a few weeks ago.” Chris answered, beaming the famous smile that made him such a magnetic personality to those who bore witness to his feats of athletic and social brilliance. “I’ve been hoping that I would run into you in one way or another once I came into the US, but I didn’t realize how big Boston was.”

“What area are you staying in? They put me with a family in Boston not too far away from here, in fact its less than 30 mins away.”

“I’m with a wonderful family in a place called Melrose, which isn’t too far from here too, but outside Boston.” Chris answered. “How about you? How’s the family you’re staying with? Are they nice?”

“They have been great to me, nwanne. I think they got us to stay with good families. I couldn’t have asked for anyone better if I’d tried. I travelled to Boston with a Ghanaian. He is also lodged in Melrose like you and is a nice guy who I’ve managed to keep contact with through the guy who picked us up at the airport. Have you met any other Africans since you arrived?”

“No, I haven’t. But I ran into someone while I was looking for the place to register. We didn’t talk much but he said he was Ghanaian too. We met not too far away from here, actually.”

They both scanned the area around them from their heightened position on the steps, looking around to see if they would catch sight of another black face in the sea of white faces that surrounded them.

“There he is!” Chris exclaimed, pointing in a direction of the building with the spire on top.
“That’s Kofi. The guy I told you I came to Boston with on the plane from New York. Well, well. It seems like we came here at about the same time. Perfect timing from all of us.”

Kofi saw their enthusiastic hand waving, and quickly cut through the crowd happy to see familiar faces. “Hi Uchechi. We finally meet again. I’m glad I’m not the only Black person here today. There are more people here than I imagined. I met Chris just a few minutes ago. Do you two know each other?”

“Yes. We come from the same town back in Eastern Nigeria.” Uchechi answered grabbing Kofi’s outstretched hand. “It seems like the two of you actually live in the same town.”

“So, it would seem.” Chris answered. “But if we can get through our registration process, we can then move on to other things.”

“True. We just have to figure out where to begin.” Uchechi said. “I was about to go up into this building to make enquires, before you called me.”

“Alright then.” Chris said as he started walking up the steps, “Let’s see what we can find out.”

The men at the reception were quite helpful and gave them directions as to what they needed to do and where to go, after which

the boys thanked them and headed out to begin what turned out to be a long and stressful day.
They found out that the University had taken measures already to ensure that their registration process went without a hitch, seemingly taking into consideration that the boys would not just be starting a new stage of education at the famous Ivy league institution, but were starting a life in not just a new country, but a new continent thousands of miles away from home.

The next thing the boys did was to go to the Freshmen Dormitories that they had been assigned to. They had found out that they had all been assigned to a group of Dorms nicknamed as the "Union Dormitories" which were just outside the famous Harvard Yard.

Uchechi had been assigned to Greenough Hall which was the closest of the Union dorms to the Harvard Yard, Kofi to Pennypacker Hall which housed the University Student-run Radio Station WHRB, while Chris was assigned to Hurlbut Hall. The latter halls both named after former luminaries at Harvard.

The three decided to accompany each other to see the places they would be residing in for the next year, starting with Kofi. Uchechi and Chris went with him to look at his new quarters. They loved the spiral staircase that wound its way up the building and around which the hall was laid out. Kofi would be sharing a large Double room with another Freshman, who wasn't yet present.

They then went on to see Hurlbut Hall, where Chris had been assigned to. Uchechi and Kofi followed Chris in to inspect his room, which turned out to be a nice single room and meant that he would have some bit of privacy to himself, Uchechi thought. The boys had crossed by some of the other halls on the Yard, which whilst great for being right in the middle of all university activity, didn't really appeal to Uchechi's sense of privacy. Kofi on the other hand, had been happy to have someone to share the rather large room, with.

"What do you think of everything we've seen so far? Kofi asked.

"The place is even more magnificent than I imagined" Uchechi answered. "I mean, look at all these magnificent buildings. Look at all the people here from different races and

countries. Everything seems steeped in history and excellence, and we get to call it home over the next four years. I can't wait to start."
"I agree, brother. It's a long way from Africa, but I feel like I'm going to love it here."

They left Hurlbut Hall after Chris had an introductory visit with the Hall Proctor, who briefed him on the things he needed to know about the freshman hall. They then proceeded to walk up to Uchechi's new place of residence, Greenough Hall.

Uchechi discovered that he too like Chris, was going to have a single room. Whilst not as big as his tribesman's, he was happy to be afforded a place where he could lay his head in relative peace, should he need the space. Just as Chris had done, he saw that the Hall Proctor was present and introduced himself, so that he could obtain any information he might need to know, before moving into the dormitory. His name was Steven Hanna, and he closed a large Bible which Uchechi could see was a King James Version.

"Hello young man. I trust you have been able to get on with the registration process without too much hassle?"

"Good afternoon, Sir." Uchechi replied. "There were young queues that we had to wait in line for, but so did everyone and it gave me a chance to meet and talk to a few people."

"That's great news." Mr. Hanna said. "You're socializing and getting used to your new environment, which will make things easier for yourself to settle in here. Are you staying a long distance away from here?" To which Uchechi answered in the negative, explaining that the train ride to the yard took only about 30 mins or so.

"Good. That should help you when you're moving your things into the house. I'll be looking forward to seeing you when you've settled in. I know this is a big change for you but we're going to do the best we can do to make it an easy and enjoyable one."

"Thank you, Sir. I'm looking forward to it myself and will move in as quickly as possible."

"Good talking to you, young man. We'll hopefully have more of an opportunity to be better acquainted after you've moved in."

"Looking forward to that. Thanks again."

With that Uchechi left the office and joined his friends outside. They took time to walk around to see the rest of the university structures and its environs, delighted at the prospect of being a part of its storied history.

As the afternoon drifted into evening, they made their way back towards the train station, having collected their individual lecture timetables and so, knowing what their routines were going to consist of for the semester. That and the knowledge of where each other's residences were going to be, they collected contact phone numbers to coordinate their arrivals into the new places of abode later that week.

Uchechi thoroughly enjoyed the trip back down the line towards what had been home to him for the better part of two months, to see the Clarkes. He reveled once again at sight of the Charles River and followed the steps back up to the ground level when he got to Andrew Station and walked back to the house on Boston Street.

Catherine was home after work. She was a journalist working with the Boston Globe and thoroughly loved her job. Uchechi loved

reading newspapers and would spend time talking about the headlines or the topics in the news with her whenever they had the time.
They had bonded well in the weeks since his arrival and he felt a good connection with her where he felt he could broach certain topics with her and get her honest opinion on matters arising.

As he walked through the door, he felt a certain pang in his chest, as he realized he's time in the Clarke household was coming to an end. He had come to consider the Clarke's as surrogate parents. The first Americans that he had grown to know, love and trust.

The Clarke's had never had any children and had come to take to Uchechi as one of their own regardless of the disparity in their race and life experiences. They had thoroughly enjoyed his stay, and Catherine had quietly started to dread the day when he might leave to go to live in his Harvard University accommodation.

"How was it at the University?" She asked. "Did everything go smoothly?"

"The place is absolutely magnificent." He replied. "There is so much history around the place, and the people were nice. Everything went well, and I also got to see a friend from back home."
"That's great to hear Uchechi. Did you have any lunch?"

"No ma'am. In all the excitement of today, we forgot to get something proper to eat. But we grabbed some snacks at a Burger shop."

"That's not food." Catherine smiled as she repeated her constant refrain about fast food. "Settle down and I'll fix you something to eat. I believe Cliff will be back in any moment now, so we can all get something to eat together."

Uchechi went on inside to drop his bag and all its contents onto the bed before returning to the kitchen to see if Catherine needed any help setting the table or anything, at which point Clifford came through the door just as Catherine had predicted he would.

She had made some Spaghetti Bolognese, and after prayers they dug into the sumptuous meal which Catherine had once again delivered with her consistently great cooking panache.

"I have something to tell you." Uchechi said as they came towards the end of the meal. "We've been assigned to our various schoolhouses of residence, and I think I will be moving in by the end of this week so I can be ready for the beginning of classes next week."
Catherine looked quietly at Clifford and said to the young man she had grown fond of.

"We've known you would eventually be going off to the University once the school opened for registration. Now, you can get to enjoy all the interesting aspects of student's life here in the United States. We're going to miss you when you go, but..." This bit said with another look towards Clifford, "We want you to know that you're welcome here, whenever you want to drop in."

"Absolutely Uche." Clifford added. "Just pop down wherever you feel the need. But even when there isn't any need, still stop over. You're very welcome here."

"Thank you so much" Uchechi said smiling a sad smile, as he realized that he was indeed going to miss his favorite American couple. "I promise I'll come down as often as I possibly can."

“You’ve got yourself a deal buddy.” Clifford replied smiling, as he looked at his wife who had a smile playing on her lips too.

Thereupon, Uchechi took the dishes off to the sink, a habit he had brought with him from across the Atlantic, helping Catherine with the clearing and washing up as he had done almost from the first day in which he had arrived.

It had not just taken the day’s events to get him to realize how much he liked his surrogate family, but right there and then, he resolved to make it a point never to let them forget how much he had cherished and appreciated all they had done and been to him in his short time there…

CHAPTER SIX

"For I know what I have planned for you" says the Lord. "I have plans to prosper you, not to harm you. I have plans to give you a future filled with hope. When you call out to me and come to me in prayer, I will hear your prayers. When you seek me in prayer and worship, you will find me available to you. If you seek me with all your heart and soul, I will make myself available to you." Says the Lord. "Then I will reverse your plight and will regather you from all the nations and all the places where I have exiled you," say the Lord. "I will bring you back to the place from which I exiled you."

As Uchechi listened to Rev. R. Jerrold Gibson gave his sermon about the promise of peace and a new future at Sunday service reading from Jeremiah 29: 11-14 at the Harvard Memorial Church, Uchechi was taken back to the services held at his home church back home in Owerri. The Sunday Service was such a huge day in the Chukwuka family, with everyone in their Sunday best, leaving at generally the same time or at least at a time early enough to ensure that they weren't late, late being making sure you were inside the church before the choir led the Church clergy into the building to the singing of hymns, signaling the commencement of the day's service. The sermons by the great Reverend Nwaozuzu in the Anglican Church were always something never to be missed…

Uchechi looked around the church, impressed not just by the architectural design of both the interior and exterior, just as he had been with most of the building on the Harvard Yard, but also with the memorials dedicated to the war dead from the World Wars, starting with the 373 that died in the first World War the catalyst for the building of the church in 1932. Uchechi greatly admired and respected the resolve to keep alive and venerate the memories of the men and women who had given their life to defend the ideals of their country, something Uchechi could empathize with as a Nigerian, as it was the failure of the British government to offer even a simple thank you or acknowledgement of the sacrifices of the thousands that died serving the British army in the 2nd World War that was the catalyst for the independence movement that was to bear fruit in weeks, back home.

Rev. Gibson had delivered a great sermon that day, a day which marked the first weekend living on campus for a lot of freshmen, including Uchechi, Chris and Kofi. He had taken the time to talk to as many of the freshmen that would wait behind after the service. When it got to Uchechi's turn, Uchechi decided that he would ask him how he was finding the position of Minister of the church, considering he had just been named as the temporary replacement for the now resigned former great Pusey Minister Rev. George A. Buttrick.

"Hello young man." The Reverend greeted him as he approached, "Good to meet you and thank you for worshipping with us today. What's your name?"

"It's Uchechi, Sir. It's great to meet you and may I say congratulations on your new position, Sir. Your sermon was great."

"The pleasure is all mine, Uchechi. Hope I got that right?" Where are you from if I may ask? This will be the first time I've heard your name, but hopefully not the last time. By the way, mine's Rev. Roland Gibson and I'm glad you enjoyed the sermon." He said with an easy smile, illuminating his face.

"You called it right, Reverend. And yes, you will definitely be seeing more of me." Uchechi replied laughing. I'm from the Eastern region in Nigeria and us as Anglicans, take the Scripture and Christianity very seriously. Today, reminded me of one more thing I miss from back home. How are you finding your new position?"

"Any opportunity to serve our Lord and bring our community even closer together in faith, is an honor worth celebrating and worth maximizing to the best of one's ability and is a pleasure." The good Reverend replied. "Hopefully, we as a community will be able to bring even more of a positive impact to this great environment that we are in. You must be among the students who have come over from West Africa. How are you finding life here in America?"

"I would have to say that God has been with me, and he has put me into the path of lot of good people, and I couldn't ask for more."

"That's great to hear, Uchechi. You'll find that this is a great place to be in, both with the community and infrastructure. Also feel free to talk to me either here or at my office if you need to talk or help on any matter. It will be my pleasure to help in whatever way that I can."

"Thank you, Reverend. Looking forward to your sermon at next week's service."

"God Bless you son, and welcome to Harvard." With that he turned his attention to the next student that was waiting to see him, while Uchechi went on to join his two friends who had already had a conversation with the Reverend.

As he came down the steps of the church towards his friends, he noticed a group of girls standing off to the side, seemingly waiting for someone coming out from the church just as he had done. There were a few other pockets of people standing around in a similar fashion including his friends, and as he passed the group of girls standing together in a group of 4, his eyes fixated on the face of a pretty girl of average height and blonde hair. He was just beginning to remark to himself as to how beautiful she looked, when her blue eyes caught him looking, bringing a smile to her lips, and she motioned towards him just as he was about to cross.

"Hey, how are you? She said, as she kept her eyes on him. "Are you a freshman too?"

The rest of her group all turned their attention towards him, while he noticed from the corner of his eye that his friends turned their gaze to the group of white girls.

"Yes, I am. I moved in this weekend. Nice to meet you. How about you? My name is Uchechi, by the way."

"Nice to meet you, Uchechi. Hope I said it that right?" She asked smiling, to which he slightly inclined his head with a little laugh.

"You were close, but at least you tried. It's your first time hearing that name and it was a good attempt."

"Well, I'd want to get better." She said laughing too. "So, tell me. How do I say it right?"

"It's U-Che-Ch-E. Uchechi. Try it."

"Uchechi!"
"That's better. You're doing well." And they both laughed.

“Well, these are my friends.” She said motioning towards the circle of girls around her, which now included the fifth member of the group, and the one they had been waiting for, who had just joined from the church. “She’s Dawn. That’s Jane, Carla and Ann.” She said pointing to each person as she revealed their names, who each in turn stretched out for a handshake with Uchechi. “My name is Mary, and it’s great to meet you. Are you African by any chance? I heard that there were a few students joining Harvard from the continent.”

“Yes, I am. I’m Nigerian to be precise, and this is a great place to be. By the way, please meet my friends.” With which he called out to his two friends. “This is Chris, a friend and a great student and athlete in our country, and this is Kofi from Ghana. We’ve all come here together.” Chris and Kofi joined the group, exchanging handshakes as everyone introduced themselves.

“A great athlete huh?” Dawn enquired smilingly as she shook hands with Chris, “They are going to love you here, if you are great at both academics and sports.” She stated matter-of-factly.

"He's going to be great." Uchechi confirmed. "Actually, he has always been."

"I think my friend is exaggerating on my behalf." Chris said smiling, speaking for the first time since being introduced. "But he's heart is in a good place."

"Dawn is going to join the Track team at Radcliffe." Mary said. "We both grew up just outside Boston. Can't wait to get started with lectures tomorrow. It seems like we have been waiting to get to university since forever!"

"Radcliffe? Is that one of the schools here?" Uchechi asked.

"No, not that." Mary answered. "It's just that for a long time, female students weren't allowed to attend Harvard. We had to attend separate college called Radcliffe. That only changed during the Second World War when the two colleges entered an arrangement, and then only formalized just a few years ago. It's only been since then that we have been able to be awarded Harvard degrees. However, the athletics departments are still separate, but hopefully even that will merge soon."

"We also have our separate places of Residence from you guys." Dawn said, chipping in. "That is, you guys stay here on the Harvard Yard, but we have to stay in the Radcliffe hostels which are further away from here."

Uchechi was familiar with single sex only schools, as he had been in one for his Secondary school education. But he had assumed, that all that would not be attainable in the University system, just as was going to be the case in the newly opened University of Nigeria in Nsukka, eastern Nigeria.

"But we will still be able to attend the same classes, right? Kofi asked.

"Absolutely Kofi." Mary replied. "Can't wait to start lectures tomorrow."

"What course are you studying?" Uchechi asked.

"I'm studying Economics. How about you?

"Mechanical Engineering"

The others offered up their courses of study as the conversation went round the assembled freshmen.

"Where are you guys off to now?" Dawn asked.

"We'll take a walk and round the Yard for a bit." Chris replied, "Then we'll go and get ourselves something to eat back at our houses. What about you ladies?"

"Probably something along those lines." Ann said.

"We need to find an ice cream shop, pronto." Mary said smiling "I guess we'll be seeing you guys around the yard then."

"Absolutely." Uchechi replied. "We'll probably attend some classes together, and so I'll be keeping any eye out, just in case." "It's been a pleasure" Chris added. "You ladies are the some of the first people that we've come to meet here. Maybe we'll all have some type of gathering one of these days."

"You'll have to tell us about that Ice cream shop when you find it." Kofi said with a laugh.

“We’ll be sure to pass on that information.” Dawn replied smiling “You can never have too much Ice cream in your life, in my experience.”

“We have a deal then.” Chris said, “Hope you girls have a great Sunday.”

With that, the two groups of freshmen exchanged goodbyes and walked off in separate directions. Uchechi and Mary briefly caught another’s eye one more time, which seemed to make her eyes seemingly break into a smile. She had one of those faces that could convey emotion through the eyes.

Uchechi smiled as he turned his attention back to his group of friends as the started walking towards Memorial Hall, the magnificent building that one of Kofi’s new housemates told him was built to honor the men who died during the American Civil War, and which served as a poignant reminder of Boston’s abolitionist stance. It also apparently used to serve as the venue for Freshman dining until a few decades earlier.

They walked down the road a little more, attracted to the magnificent facade of the

Edward Mallinckrodt Chemical Laboratory, which was also going to be the building that Kofi was going to spend a lot of time in, as it was the building that housed the Chemistry faculty, the course that Kofi was studying for.

The three West African Harvard freshmen then turned around to go back towards their Dormitories, so that they could relax for a bit and then meet up to go to the Harvard Union, or Freshman Union as some would call it, which was where they as Freshman were assigned to get their meals, unless they were friends with an Upperclassman who could invite them into the Houses of Residence for meals.

"Did you take a look at the menu at the Union before we left?" Chris asked his friends, as they made their way through the Yard.

"Not really." Uchechi answered. "But breakfast was great. I've come to like those pieces of beef they call sausages here."

"Don't forget the baked beans" Kofi chimed in. "Apparently it's a Boston specialty."

"They cook really well here." Chris said. "I'm going to need to watch my weight." He said laughing. "I'm signing up for their football and athletic programs when they officially open school on Monday, tomorrow. Apparently, we as freshmen, don't get to join the main sports teams for the university. We will compete in a freshman category until we are through with this academic year. After that, we can now join the full-fledged academic program in all their sports."

"They call football, soccer here." Uchechi remarked. "It's definitely a lot different from the game we all love back home, and for a game they call football, there doesn't seem to be much contact of the said ball with their feet!"

"I noticed that too." Kofi said laughing. "But they seem to really love the game and go all out when playing. Both men and women, young and old, everyone is into the game."

"I think the biggest game in the country, is the one that you see all the kids playing in the fields with each other, and also with their fathers." Chris said. "The one they Baseball. It bears some resemblance to the game of cricket that the English brought to Africa but seems a lot more exciting and dynamic."

"The one that has really caught my fancy is Basketball." Uchechi said, "But good height seems to be a needed advantage to really excel at it."

"They have a great selection of truly great games to play, and the facilities to match." Kofi said.

"Facilities. Infrastructure. Those are the two things Africa needs to build up." Uchechi opined. "If we as a continent can get our objectives right on those two things in particular, it will help solve a lot of the developmental problems in our various countries."

"Hear, hear" Chris said in the mannerism of colonial era Brits, causing a burst of laughter from the group as they remembered the regular comedic sketches back home of their soon-to-be former colonizers.
They had been walking down Boylston Street, taking in the bustle on one of the major streets in the Harvard/Cambridge area which ran along the sides of the grounds accommodating the various Houses of Residence and other Harvard faculty

buildings, fields and Dormitories, down towards the Charles River.

"Well, guess it's time to discover what they have in store for us for lunch." Chris said as turned left onto the road leading to the Houses of Residence and then the Freshman Halls, with his being among the first amongst the young group of West Africans.

"Unfortunately, I doubt there will be sausages involved." Uchechi said, to which the group started laughing again.

"I can see that I'll have to keep an eye out for you because of this sausage matter." Chris said smiling. "I'll tell you what, why don't we arrange to have a morning run to start the day, every day. That way, we'll all keep fit, especially as we are all going to be enjoying the novelties of our new meal plans, it would seem".

"That sounds like a great idea." Kofi replied. "I'm going to try out for the sprint teams. Those early morning runs will only help".

"Maybe, not on Sunday's though." Uchechi said. "We fully rest on the seventh day, just as Our Lord."

“Just say you don’t want to run on Sunday’s”. Chris remarked with a laugh. “No need to bring Our Lord into this matter!”. This, sparking another round of laughter out of the group.

They were still laughing when they got to Eliot House, another one of Harvard’s beautifully designed buildings, with its iconic Roof tower adorning the massive complex.

“That will be great place to live.” Chris said. “I’ve heard that it’s a great House to be a part of.”

“That’s what Ed, my roommate said as well.” Kofi said. “They apparently are quite picky with the upperclassmen they admit.”

“How are you finding your new roommate?” Uchechi asked. “What’s he like?”

“He’s a nice guy, actually. His family only recently came over here from Ireland, but they live in Philadelphia. He’s new to the area too, so we are both exchanging information on all the things we know.”

“It sounds like you’ve found yourself a good friend there.” Chris said. “I think as we get to move around more, the more people we're going to start to interact with."

"I know. Just look at the way we met those girls today." Uchechi agreed.

"Ahh. The girls." Chris said smiling. "I'd almost forgotten about that earlier. You seem to have already got the ball rolling when it comes to girlfriends."

"And she looks good too." Kofi added. "What was her name again, Maggy?"

"Mary." Uchechi replied, laughing. "That was just good luck that she happened to be waiting for her friend, at the same time as you guys were waiting for me. And don't pretend, you didn't like the look of Dawn. I swear I caught you two looking at each other."

"I'm surprised you even noticed." Chris laughed. "I was almost certain you were being hypnotized by those blue eyes."

"So, you noticed her eyes, too?" Kofi interjected, and then turning to Uchechi with a laugh, "This man is greedy." He continued, pointing at Chris. "He was looking at two of them, at the same time!"

"Look at you, pretending to be innocent in the matter." Chris replied, "You think I didn't catch you looking at Ann?"

The freshmen were laughing loudly now, as they navigated the pathways between the various houses. They had almost circled round their dormitories in their bid to see more of Boylston Street, and because of that, the freshman dormitories of Chris and Kofi were the first to be approached by the group. After they had decided on when they were going to congregate and where, for their trip to Harvard Union for lunch, they went their separate ways.

CHAPTER SEVEN

"Happy Independence Day, guys! Congratulations Nigeria!"

The party at Harvard celebrating Nigeria getting its Independence from the British on October 1st, 1960, was celebrated in style on the Harvard Yard with as great a boisterous atmosphere as could be put together by the Nigerian students resident in the Harvard area.

They were joined by a cross section of Harvard students across all the classes at the historic institution; friends, roommates, housemates, course mates and the curious others wondering what the party was all about and joining to find out. What students would miss the chance to attend any party? Not too many.
Even better, the historic day had fallen on a Saturday, the perfect day for a weekend party after a full week of lectures, coursework and assignments.

For Chris and Uchechi, it was a day to savor, having been witnesses to some of the campaigns run by the political parties and pressure groups to make that day a reality. They could only imagine the celebrations that were going on back home, celebrations marking the end of a struggle that seemed to march to the sound of the boots of the unheralded men returning from lands far from theirs, leaving behind the bodies of thousands of their friends, fighting for the freedoms of countries that had never bothered to acknowledge or thank them at the end of the 2nd World War.

The Igbo boys would have given anything to be present for those parties and the fulfillment of a dream and struggle that had lasted 15 years. It was yet another moment in their sojourn to America, where they missed home and would give anything to be among family and friends during this great moment.

Filling in as substitutes for the family they longed to have close, where the friends that they had made in the short few weeks of their time at Harvard. Standing off to the side were the group of girls that they had met at the Memorial Church only a few weeks ago. Mary had brought Dawn, Ann and the rest of her crew down from their hostel to join their new West African friends, on this great day.

Mary and Uchechi had now met a few times since that day at the bottom of the Memorial steps. Mutual classes, as well as a couple of group meetings at the freshman common with the rest of their respective groups.

Moving around the various groups of people at the party with his roommate Ed, and of course cheerfully telling everyone that he could find that his country had achieved the same thing three years earlier, was of course the other West African of the trio, Kofi.

“Congratulations guys.” He said approaching his Nigerian friends with a smile on his face. “Better late than never!”

“Oh, shut up” Uchechi replied laughing. “What have you achieved with the three-year head start? We’ll soon start beating you guys in all areas of development.”

“Not at football, though” Kofi said with a sly look in Chris’ direction.

“Oh, please.” Chris replied laughing. “That was just one game.” And then with a look towards Ed, who had followed his roommate over, “He’s referring to the great rivalry our two countries have in soccer.”

“Come back to me when you guys start winning the matches.”

“Don’t worry.” Uchechi said with a laugh. “You won’t dampen our day, and we’ll remember this boasting the next time we play each other.”

The party went on into the night as the students all celebrated a day in what had turned out to be a banner year for African countries seeking independence from the colonial era powers, Great Britain and France. A total of 17 African countries would have achieved by the time the year of 1960 would end.

That year, 1960, was also to prove to be a memorable year in the United States, and even more memorable to the Harvard community, for the year was an election year in the country, and an alumnus of the great institution was one of the two candidates competing to get the job of being the most powerful and influential man on earth, the President of the United States. His name was John F. Kennedy.

John Fitzgerald Kennedy, or JFK as he was popularly known, was a politician from a great Massachusetts family who had graduated from Harvard 20 years ago, back in 1940. He and his elder brother Joseph Junior, who too had graduated from oldest and most prestigious university in the United States, had gone off to war in Europe and the Asia Pacific in the most destructive conflict the world had ever seen against the Axis Powers -Germany, Italy and Japan.

They both served heroically in World War II, with John earning a Purple Heart for his bravery in the Pacific, but tragically, his elder brother was killed in action over the English Channel, an event that was to change the trajectory of John's life.

Upon his return to the United States, he was encouraged by his father to venture into politics, a path that had previously been proposed for his late elder brother, Joseph Junior. John being the second eldest son of his illustrious father Joe, was thus thrust forward into the political limelight, first as Massachusetts Representative to Congress in 1946, and then after three successful terms in the United States Congress, he defeated the Republican incumbent to begin a historically successful first of two terms as a United States senator in 1952, all funded by his father.

Whilst he narrowly lost out to being the Democratic Vice-Presidential pick during the party convention at Chicago in 1956, he had gained valuable national exposure, putting him in good position to run for the 1960 Presidential election, which would also mean he wouldn't be running against an incumbent, as the ever-popular Allied Supreme Commander and War hero turned politician Dwight Eisenhower, would be leaving office having served his two terms in office.

All this led into the pivotal Presidential elections that were to hold on November 8, 1960, against another veteran from World War II who had returned from the war, entered politics and won election to serve as a United States Congressman in 1946, just as JFK had done himself, and the serving Vice President of the United States, Richard Nixon.

The wave of independence celebrations happening across the African continent in 1960, was not the only society-changing phenomenon that was grabbing the news headlines at the time. The United States was also coming to grips with the Civil Rights movement that had begun to gain momentum through the 1950's with the emergence of figures like Martin Luther King and Malcolm X, a fight to bring about equal rights for the African-American population of the United States, rights that had been given every other American, but had so far, thanks to Slavery and then the Reconstruction period after the American Civil War, been denied to African-Americans.

There had been various forms of protest used by the different Civil Rights groups to fight against the various societal instruments of Segregation, Discrimination and Racism. So, in 1960, a protest movement started by three North Carolina A&T students at a Woolworths in Greensboro, North Carolina, Joseph McNeil, Franklin McCain, Ezell Blair Jr., and David Richmond, began in February of that year, a sit-in campaign to protest against the store's (and company's) policy of not serving Black people at the lunch counter.

By October of that year, the sit-in protests had spread across the nation and especially in the South, and not just with Black people from all walks of life joining the protest, but also White Americans joining the protests in solidarity with their fellow citizens, to push for what was right.

On one of their meetings at the Harvard Union, Carl, an African-American freshman who had grown up in Boston, and had befriended Uchechi due to the fact that their dorm rooms were opposite one another, ensuring that they tended to head out to classes on the Yard at about the same time, had told his Nigerian friend of the sit-in protests organized by Harvard students in the Boston area under the group called the Emergency Public Integration Committee (EPIC), led by graduate students Michael L. Walzer and Harvey Pressman, against the local Woolworth's but which had minimal impact on either the local or student population at the time.

"Imagine that happening to us here." Carl remarked. "Some things in the world just make no sense. We are all the same people, have never understood why people discriminate or hate people they don't know".

The student population was especially enthusiastic about the fact that one of their own, an alum who had walked through the same halls that they had done and lived in the same accommodation, not to mention the fact that he was a local, brought up in

Massachusetts as he was, was running to be President. The Democratic Party student arm on campus, The Young Democrats and their conservative rivals, The Young Republicans, engaged in a battle of wills to see who could pull their candidate to win the highest seat in the land. The young liberals had the decided advantage due to the local and national popularity of their candidate, that as well as the fact that he would be the youngest elected President in United States history if he won, a fact not lost on his young supporters and admirers.

On October 19th, 1960, the momentum of the Civil Rights sit-in campaigns protesting Segregation in the South, and the Presidential Campaign and historical political accent of John F. Kennedy became entwined.

Martin Luther King Jnr along with about 50 other protesters, was arrested in the city of Atlanta, Georgia for participating in a sit-in demonstration against the segregationist lunch counter policy of a department store called Rich's.

After the group of protesters refused to leave the department store, they were arrested on a newly passed law from that year which allowed for the prosecution of any person refusing to leave private property, a now new misdemeanor offence.

Charges were dropped against quite a few of the other protesters, but Rev. King was charged with a more serious crime of having his arrest violate the terms of a previous state probation from earlier that same year. He was then sentenced to six months with hard labor in one of the most outrageous miscarriages of justice seen, but one that was largely symbolic of that era, and in truth for African Americans, a reality of the American justice system from before that time, and after.
This judgment however, caused a furor in the American judicial and political landscape.

John F Kennedy, in the middle of a tight presidential campaign against Richard Nixon, his early gains from the first televised political debate slowly being whittled away, and as the popular sitting President Eisenhower began to get more involved in the Republican effort to retain the presidency, decided to become involved in the case, against the advice of several of his advisers who asked him not to get involved in the murky affair down south.

He called the Governor of Georgia, Ernest Vandiver, a fellow Democrat and a supporter of his presidential bid to see what could be done on the 26th after the Civil Rights Leader was put in a Maximum-Security prison, and then the wife of the Civil Rights leader, Coretta King, to find out how he could help in the matter. He had used his contacts and profile in both the Democratic party and in American politics, to leverage his influence with people involved with the case in Atlanta, and subsequently MLK was released on October 27th.

The African American community did not forget, and less than two weeks later, on November 8th, 1960, John Kennedy won perhaps the closest election victory in United States history, helped in retrospect by the African American vote heavily swinging in the final days of the campaign towards the Massachusetts Senator in the Northern states of the country, giving JFK the slight margins of victory there, enough to blunt the late momentum of Nixon's campaign.

On the Harvard Yard, the celebrations were everywhere, as both the students who felt a kinship with the young Senator and the staff of the institution; a lot of whom knew quite a few of the advisers to the campaign, with the Massachusetts native taking a lot of his team from the Harvard Yard community, joined in hopeful expectation of the inspirational scion of the Kennedy clan and alum, who was going to be the first President of the country born in the 20th Century.

Just as there had been just a month prior during the Nigerian Independence Day celebrations, there were pop up parties around the Yard bringing out the Uchechi and his friends to bask in the euphoria of the day. The year 1960 was turning out to be quite the year of change not just on the African continent, but also in the most influential country in the world.

That year was also the beginning of something special at Harvard, albeit one of a more individual nature, as the freshman sports seasons kicked off across the state and the Ivy League, the historically affluent, elite classification of universities that Harvard, Yale, Cornell, Dartmouth, Columbia, Brown, Princeton and the University of Pennsylvania belonged to.

Chris Ohiri, the brilliant Nigerian sports star from Owerri whose exploits back on the continent Uchechi was all too familiar with, decided it was time to announce his presence to the Harvard Yard community. Everyone, faculty members, students, coaches and fans of all sports became aware of the prodigious talents of the young West African of Igbo extraction.

Maybe it was that he fractured the goalkeeper's wrists with a shot during his very first football/soccer game against the MIT, and scored in every fashion possible, dribbling and out thinking his adversaries to the admiration of teammates, fans and opponents, or maybe it was the sheer ludicrousness of him repeating his scoring brilliance against his team's opponents in the very next game.

Or maybe it was the fact that he also excelled at both Track & Field events as well, dominating every event that he took part in, and just as he was doing at the same time on the soccer field, breaking and setting new records with each passing day.

Uchechi basked in the burgeoning celebrity of his friend, proud of his achievements just as if there were his own. In his mind, there could be no greater ambassador of his people, especially in their abilities and potential, than his great friend.

On their way home to their dorms from the grounds down on Boylston Road, he noticed that everyone wanted to know who the young Nigerian was. They walked home with the group, which included Uchechi, Kofi and his roommate Ed, Mary, Dawn and their group of friends, asking his take on “that move” or “that goal” which they had witnessed with their own eyes, and were so taken with the brilliance of the moment, that they wanted to know what exactly had inspired such excellence.

As Uchechi watched such scenes play out again and again, he was struck by how those instances mirrored other occasions that he had observed back home in Owerri. Everyone, both young and old knew they were watching something great take place back there, and it seemed that despite the change in continents, time zones, people and country, Chris’ brilliance still had the same effect it had on people. Great in Nigeria, was great in America. Whatever ethnicity or country, good people recognized and appreciated great feats and great people

when they saw them and acknowledged them as such.
For a young black man like Uchechi, a foreigner in a country with headlines of racial injustice playing out on the media headlines and in society, it gave him hope that despite the tragedy of those happenings, there was a pathway to success in that country, that the vagaries of prejudice might not be able to extinguish.

He could be as great as he wanted to be.

Thus, went their freshman year. The great uncertainty of their foray into a new country, people and culture, had produced a realization of their potential and the currency that it could afford them in their everyday life, which in turn greatly increased their levels of confidence and determination to succeed.

In every sphere possible.

CHAPTER EIGHT

The summer holidays of 1961 went by rather quickly, as good times tend to do. Uchechi had stayed at the home of the Clarke's for the entirety of the break between his freshman year and sophomore turn.

The Clarkes had been happy to have him stay over for that summer. Trips to the city center with Catherine including an especially delightful trip to see some of Boston's historic drinking places. While neither was a drinker, she had come to know Uchechi well enough in the year since she had first seen him, that he loved history, culture and old buildings, things that Boston had by the truckload.

From the Green Dragon in which a lot of the American Revolution was planned, as well as the Boston Tea Party, and from where Paul Revere was famously reputed to have taken off to warn of the incoming British forces, to the Warren Tavern which boasted as among its clientele George Washington, Commander of the Revolutionary forces and first President of the United States.

Uchechi lapped up the history tour lessons, luxuriating in the opportunity to immerse himself in the traditions and culture of the great old city. It was one of the things that had helped him settle quicker than he would have thought at Harvard Yard. Whilst he was living in a foreign land, far from the homeland he had spent all his life in, he had always been drawn to the traditions and culture of other places, and the sheer amount of history that he lived and walked through every day at Harvard, had turned out to be rather comforting to him.

Back home, culture, tradition and history were at the forefront of every aspect of life. That sentiment was proudly preserved, cherished and appreciated in every corner of the land, which to Uchechi, made life infinitely more interesting, a treasure and a mystery of origins to be discovered and uncovered among the different peoples that inhabited the country of Nigeria.

That same comfort and interest in history and tradition that he was used to back in his homeland, was quite evident in the city of Boston, which brought a feeling of familiarity, and allowed him settle in faster that he thought he would have, before he got to land at the city that birthed the American Revolution.

Clifford would also take him to see the other great tradition that had captured the pride and imagination of the Boston public of the day, albeit a more modern one, the Boston Celtics.

The team coached by Red Auerbach and led by a bevy of great players like the legendary Bill Russell, Sam Jones and Bob Cousy, the prior two being African American, had been on a tear through the American Basketball landscape, winning championship after championship in the National Basketball Association.

With the other popular Boston team, The Red Sox of Major League Baseball, amid a decades long championship slump going back 40 years, the city had gravitated to the title winning Basketball team.

Clifford would take Uchechi to the famous Boston Garden Stadium to watch those legendary Celtics play, showcasing their championship winning pedigree. From the indomitable presence and tenacity of their Centre, Bill Russell to the wizardry of the Point Guard, Bob Cousy, “the Garden” was a permanent cacophony of noises of admiration of some sort of skill, or derision of their opponents, with one chant or the other building up together with the ebb and flow of the game.

The atmosphere at that temple of Basketball perfection was something Uchechi was going to become accustomed to as he began the second of his four-year stay at Harvard, as his friend Chris was about to become unleashed on unsuspecting opponents and adoring fans alike, of the Harvard Soccer team named the Crimson, in his first season with the team, as freshman were not allowed to be a part of the main University sports teams.

First though, as the former freshmen arrived to begin their sophomore year at the venerable Cambridge institution, Uchechi and his fellow West African mates moved into the main houses of residence, the first signal of the change in their status as they began their stint as Upperclassmen at Harvard.

Chris was accepted into Eliot House under the University appointed House Master John Finley who had high standards that had to be met for anyone wanting to be resident in the House.
The students that were a part of Eliot house, had a reputation for being highly intellectual

with a penchant for classical Shakespearean-like, Victorian era Old English mannerisms.

Master Finley insisted that the House be run with precision, which meant that food was served at the right times, the House library had such a reputation that students from other houses, would be frequently seen there studying amongst themselves.

Also, the House members had a reputation for being great athletes, something that allowed Chris to fit right in, as his record-breaking freshman exploits preceded him wherever he went.

Kofi was posted to Dunster House, named after the man Henry Dunster, who arrived in Cambridge in the mid-17th Century, and would go on to become the first President of the then fledgling Harvard College. His House Master was Gordon Fair.

Uchechi was sent to Quincy House under Master John Bullitt which been built only two years prior in 1959.

This house was the epicenter of all political activity on the Yard. It seemed that virtually every political movement was headquartered there, thanks to the Upperclassmen who were resident in the newly built accommodation.

They came from all spectrums of activity and political movement; The Young Democrats, fresh off the euphoria of the election of their favorite alum as President of the nation, The Young Republicans fighting to remain relevant and win new members in the face of their electoral defeat a year prior, and a rapidly growing progressive political landscape amongst others.

The House members also seemed to be at the forefront of different protest movements that were forming around the country at the time, be it the sit-in protests of the previous year or the Freedom Riders movement protesting the segregation of buses that had gained prominence that year of 1961.

It was a house that was to have a profound impact on Uchechi's view of America and his knowledge of the power of protesting against unfairness in society, and for change in the attitudes of people to one another.

He and Mary also became more of an item as they proceeded through the autumn of '61. They had become study partners as their freshman year progressed, and by the time they had broken for their summer recess, they had become an identifiable item on the Yard.

As they moved into their sophomore year, they began to move further into their respective courses of study; Mechanical Engineering for Uchechi and Economics for Mary, but it didn't stop them from finding time to do some "study prep" to "keep the brain cells sharp" or whatever lies they kept telling themselves in order to find the time to be together. Soon enough, they had moved past the lunch and dinner dates at the Common, as well as the study sessions at the various libraries, to discovering private "hidden" spots across the Yard and spending time at their various residencies when the opportunity presented itself.

This day however, they and the rest of the crew, Dawn, Kofi, Ann et al, were headed to the soccer field to watch the second game of Chris Ohiri's Harvard Soccer team, the Crimson, home debut.

It was the first home game of the season for the Crimson, coming only 3 days after the legendary game that Chris had played at the home of Tufts University, where the

Harvard team had won 5-0 with Chris scoring all five goals in a rout of their bewildered opponents, with the talented Nigerian seemingly dribbling and melting past his markers with ease, and scoring with devastating accuracy.

He had brought his freshman reputation for smashing in goals with either foot, along with him to his sophomore bow. By now the reputation for his shots dislocating opposing goal keepers' wrists, was well known around the Harvard Yard.
His opponents from Tufts had seemingly not done their due diligence of scouting the Owerri born West African.

The opponents for the day were another Ivy League school, Cornell University which was based in New York State.

The Soccer field while not as magnificent has the American Football field where the Harvard Crimson played, had a crowd surrounding the field which was five people deep, as all the seats had been taken in the frenzy to have the best view of the match, and Chris Ohiri in particular.
The story of his 5-goal season debut, away to Tufts had careened off every corner of the Harvard Yard, and as such, the student

population; even the ones who weren't really into sports, had come down Boylston Street to see the great, young Nigerian.

He didn't disappoint.

Uchechi and Mary had managed to secure a spot close to the halfway line, from where Uchechi had assured her that they would catch every kick of the match, virtually unhindered.

Harvard had a well-balanced team that year, built had around the smooth talents of Billy Ward, Tony Davies and Emmanuel Boyo who ran the midfield "engine room" of the Harvard Crimson.

What the crowd witnessed, was a historically great game, not just from the Igbo phenom, but also from a sensational Harvard Soccer team, perhaps gingered on by a desire to show that their five-goal masterclass in the previous game was no fluke.

Uchechi had found it difficult to sit on the ground like a few of the other students around him, including some of Mary's friends who had joined them to watch the game, but a few minutes after the game started, nobody remembered why they had wanted to sit in the first place.

The home team would score four goals by half-time in an utterly dominant display, with Chris scoring three of them, one of them so incredible and awe inspiring that people could be heard cheering from the top of the nearby Harvard Stadium when the uproar amongst the ever-increasing number of student spectators at the field, had died down.
Chris had just cut through the shell-shocked and hapless Cornell, once again.

Harvard would eventually score nine goals in that game, an Ivy league record, in an utterly rampant 9-1 shellacking of Cornell, and Chris had matched his tally of 5 goals from the Tufts game, including an occurrence in the later stages of the game that would bolster his burgeoning legend across the Harvard Yard.

One of his ferocious shots had forced the Cornell goalkeeper to depart the game with a sprained wrist, in his attempt to save the goal bound shot. Chris Ohiri had scored his 5 goals in every way possible; left foot, right foot, headers, breakaways, in didn't matter. As the students celebrated the famous and historic, on their way back to dorms and houses; Uchechi was especially happy, not just because of the performance of his fellow tribesman and close friend, but also because Mary had kept giving him kisses every time Harvard scored, oblivious to everyone around them.

An ecstatic Uchechi alongside with Kofi, Mary, Dawn and a few others walked Chris back towards the Eliot House, with shouts of acknowledgement coming from every corner, as well as steady murmurings of awe and appreciation of the young Nigerian, in same way that he had observed of that other New England based magician of an athlete, Bob Cousy…

CHAPTER NINE

Harvard Yard was abuzz with excitement as Uchechi and Mary made their way through the area on their way to the Harvard Square Theatre, to catch a Gina Lollobrigida double feature that Friday night.

Uchechi had made his way to Mary's room excitedly, as this was to be their first cinema date, one that they had planned as soon as Mary had realized that the hit movie, Come September starring her favorite actor Rock Hudson alongside the aforementioned great Italian actress, was being shown at the cinema which overlooked Harvard Square by way of Massachusetts St, in an obvious bid to not only bring in audiences for one the hit movies of 1961 but also admirers of the screen icon that Lollobrigida was.

The palpable excitement amongst students at the great University though, had more to do with the coming game against Amherst the next day, which was coming on the back of the awe-inspiring victories from the two previous meetings to start the season, as well as the blistering, jaw dropping performances of the team's star player Chris Ohiri.

However, unlike the previous game against Cornell, the coming match would be played at Amherst's turf, and Uchechi and Mary wouldn't be in attendance, leaving them to fill in their weekend with whichever activity that they pleased.

Uchechi had been to the movies with Clifford and Catherine, but had never seen a movie starring either Rock Hudson, whom he thought with a wry smile to himself as they walked to the cinema, was probably very handsome with the way Mary went on excitedly about his movies, or Gina Lollobrigida whom he knew to be beautiful thanks to the posters on the wall of Carl's room; his friend whom he had moved with from Greenough Hall that was just a walkthrough down from his; which included pictures of other great screen sirens of the day, Marilyn Monroe Dorothy Dandridge, Lena Horne and Diahann Carroll.

Carl was coming to the cinema too but had decided not to come with Uchechi as his West African friend came through to his room looking sharp in his coat, shirt and jeans, because he wanted to allow the blossoming couple their personal space so they could have the evening together. He had known about, and eventually met the beautiful Mary during freshman year, when he and Uchechi had lived in the Greenough hostel and were planning a double date the next week with his girlfriend Angie, who was studying at UMass, the University of Massachusetts in Boston.

"You're not coming down with us?" Uchechi asked, as he came to a stop at the foot of Carl's bed. The two had grown close during freshman year, with Uchechi finding him a great educator on the happenings in the African-American community, their lives, challenges and history, not just because the Civil Rights movement was exploding across the United States, but also because he knew that continental Africans and Africans in the diaspora; whether in the United States, the Caribbean or South America, were really all brothers, sisters and cousins separated by the abominable and tragic transatlantic slave trade.
He and Carl had developed a kinship after they kept bumping into one another and at the Greenough entrance…

"No brother. You two get out there and have fun." Carl said smiling. "I'll catch up with you guys at the cinema. If you'll notice me, that is".

“Knock it off” Uchechi said laughing as he turned to leave, “You’re just describing yourself when you’re with Angie. Talking of Angie, aren’t you taking her to see the film?”

“She’s working the late shift tonight at the bar. She doesn’t usually do Fridays, but an extra shift became available, and they offered it to her. We need that green, to be!”, Carl said, smiling at that final sentence taping an imaginary pocket on the side of his white briefs.

“Absolutely brother. Greet her for me when next you see her. Let me go stroll over and pick Mary from Radcliffe. Catch you later.”

With a final wave, Uchechi set off to pick up his date for the evening, skipping down the stairs to the entrance and down the street towards the Radcliffe quadrangle area. Mary had wanted to come down and meet him halfway, but he had insisted on coming to pick her up, as he always enjoyed walking and talking with her.

The movie double-feature was meant to start at 6pm, with a 45-minute break in between the two films, and Uchechi got to North House, Mary’s Radcliffe residence by 5pm.

He loved the magnificence of the North House structure whenever he went there. It looked like a building fit for a Queen, with its beautiful brown façade and tower rising up from its center, its beauty only bested by the damsel he came to see.

She was ready by 5:15 and they made the 20-minute walk down to the cinema on Church Street with time to spare and chose what treats they wanted to have while watching the film event. They both went for hotdogs with Mary getting a Crush Strawberry while Uchechi had his with an Orange Crush. After deciding to also add popcorn to their order, they sat down to wait for showtime.

Dawn, Carla and their boyfriends had also come to the cinema to catch the film features. Uchechi didn't really know the guys but had seen them around Harvard Yard and guessed they were also students at his university and exchanged pleasantries with them.

Mary, Dawn and Carla in the meantime furiously caught up on the day's events, having stayed as close as they were the first time Uchechi had seen the group outside the Harvard Memorial Church, that fateful day.

Whilst they had moved into different houses at Radcliffe, with the school residential system re-organized that year, with Dawn and Carla moving to East House, and Jane and Ann staying at North House with Mary, the group still made sure to spend as much time as they had in their freshman year.

The girls excitedly shifted their conversation to the stars of the film they were about to watch. In addition to Rock Hudson, who all the girls adored with the tall, rugged look he had, and Gina Lollobrigida whom Carla with her Italian roots, adored, there was a guy who had all the girls talking, and as if on cue, the song “Dream Lover” began playing around the ticket hall.

“Oh, my Gawd” Mary exclaimed as virtually everyone began humming the hit song, “Can’t wait to see Bobby Darin. It’s his first ever movie role too. He always looks and sounds great on television.”

“And Sandra Dee, too” Dawn added excitedly. “I’ve loved her since I first saw her in Imitation of Life.”

“That was a great film, Dawn!” Mary exclaimed. “Have you seen that movie, Uche?”

Hearing her say “Uche”, made him smile. They had eventually settled on the short form version of his name, as their relationship had gotten stronger and more intimate, as time passed.

“No, I haven’t”. I’ve seen a few movies since coming over, but not that one.”

“What was the first movie you ever saw in the cinema, after you came here?” Carla asked.

“It was a movie Clifford and Catherine, the family that first welcomed me to Boston, took me to last year. It was called The Angry Silence, starring Richard Attenborough and Pier Angeli. Great movie!”

“Wow!” Carla exclaimed. “You saw a movie with Pier Angeli, the great and magnificently beautiful Italian actress. I missed seeing that movie when it came out. What did you think of Pier?” Carla made this enquiry with a wink and smile in Mary’s direction, an exaggerated gesture that made everyone in the group burst out laughing.

“I thought she was great in the role” Uchechi said, and then with an equally exaggerated motion towards his girlfriend, "And of course, very beautiful, just like the real-life movie star I'm getting to hang out with tonight."

The group all playfully made cooing sounds as the Mary pecked him on the cheek.

"So would you say Pier Angeli's the prettiest actress you've seen in a movie?" Dawn asked.

"Probably. I haven't seen a movie with Marilyn Monroe or Dorothy Dandridge yet, even though I've seen their posters plastered on the walls of friends' rooms." This prompting laughter from the girls and guys assembled, "so yes, I'd have to say she is."

"Well," Mary said, as she led him towards the cinema with the film feature about ten mins away and ushers calling for tickets, "You're in for a treat tonight. You're about to see your second beautiful Italian actress tonight. Gina Lollobrigida's face is known across the world."

"Don't pretend you're here just for me." Uchechi said laughing as they walked towards the screen, from where they'd be watching the feature. "You're also here to see Rock Hudson and Bobby Darin. I've heard nothing else from you, but rave reviews of those two."

"Actually", Mary replied laughing and then with a coy smile said, "There IS something for you here tonight." Then, she looked away laughing and the silent question posed by Uchechi's quizzical look at her as they took their seats.

Come September, turned out to be as great a movie as Mary had thought it would be. From the opening scenes with Gina Lollobrigida's character appearing to be absolutely hypnotized by Rock Hudson's voice, to the hilarious scenes at the villa involving the Butler, Sandra Dee's group of friends and their chaperone and the marauding group of besotted boys led by Bobby Darin, the movie goers absolutely loved it, laughing and gesticulating for the entire length of the film, with girls, including Mary edging closer to their dates during the scene involving Bobby Darin performing the song "multiplication".

Even before that scene, Uchechi had begun to understand Mary's earlier coy statement about the night. As Gina slipped her foot along Rock Hudson's leg onscreen, he felt

Mary's foot, from its position where she had crossed her legs with his hand on her knee, begin to run along his leg also, gripping his hand with a slight smile on her face, whilst avoiding making eye contact with him.
He enjoyed every second of it.

Everyone was talking to each other about the movie once the credits had begun to run onscreen as the feature ended. There was to be a 20-minute interlude between the first and second feature films, and they all emptied out into the lobby to grab more snacks and drinks. Some had only wanted to watch "Come September" and left the cinema to either go home or further explore whatever else the night had to offer.

Uchechi and Mary spent the interlude necking outside, just round the corner from the main entrance. There had been much hand holding and stolen kisses during the movie as the emotional and romantic scenes came and went. She had thoroughly enjoyed the movie, and quite frankly so had he. Some of the scenes between Hudson and the amorous group of boys had reminded him of some similar happenings back home. But even more, he had enjoyed the feeling of having her so close whilst looking absolutely bewitching and captivating, and was absolutely looking forward to the second movie in the double feature.

They quickly went back into the cinema just as the United Artists trademark logo came onscreen, wielding a fresh box of popcorn and drinks as they got into their seats.

Solomon and Sheba had a completely different tone to the previous feature, with the only similarity between the two being the beautiful Gina Lollobrigida. Uchechi however, quickly settled into the movie, appreciating the biblical and religious storytelling themes on display of which he had grown up with, even though he could see some of the exaggerations to the story of Solomon that he knew so well.

The only thing that bothered him, was why Mary had wanted him to take her to see this movie, one she had seen before as it had first come out two years previous, in 1959. She seemed to particularly have wanted him to see this movie, even more than the first one which had only been released to cinema a couple of months and which she hadn't seen.

Could it be the religious tone of the movie? Sure, she knew of his religious upbringing, as he had spoken about with her when they both exchanged stories of their upbringing and life before Harvard, but for a date night movie, that was supposed to be a romantic? He wasn't quite sure if it had been a great choice and the movie's early scenes rolled by onscreen, but thought he'd go with it anyway and say nothing. Afterall, it was still time spent in close proximity to the most beautiful girl in all of Boston.

The film slowly progressed to its central theme, the growing closeness and romance between Yul Brynner's Solomon and Lollobrigida's Queen of Sheba, and just as slowly, he felt Mary's hand begin to travel between his hand, arm, chest and thigh.

Then as a scene of a Sheban religious festival with the aforementioned Queen of Sheba dancing seductively with seemingly wild abandon filling the cinema screen. Mary quietly shifted out from her seat and onto him in his seat with nary a sound made, or a word to him, and began furtively replicating the dance moves of the delectable Lollobrigida from the onscreen spectacle.

The room was of course quite dark meaning that no one else could see, enthralled as they all were to the scene playing out in front of them, but even more importantly, not many had stayed for the second feature but for a few diehard fans of the film or actors, especially as it wasn't a new release.

As Mary did her furtive dance, a naughty side of her that he hadn't seen before, comprehension slowly dawned on an ecstatic Uchechi. This was why she had wanted him to see this movie with her, a movie she herself had already seen. He also finally understood the coy look in her eye and the laugh when she had told him before they took their seats for the first feature, that there was something in the night for him as well as there was for her…

None of them said a word or made any attempt to disengage from their joined position even after the scene was over, and as the movie took a decidedly serious tone. They both lingered together for an extra minute as the lights came back on as the credits rolled onscreen, and then smiling with hands held tight, exited the cinema and into the night.

In the time that they had known each other, they had not made the leap to being intimate, not with both being of strong religious upbringing and moral compasses stuck on true north. But as the gathering darkness enveloped its newly discovered lovers, welcoming them to its protective bosom, Uchechi understood the true intention of their date night.

She had wanted him to know that she was ready, and she wanted to know too if he was ready.

Comprehension slowly dawned on an ecstatic Uchechi…and the comprehension was good…

CHAPTER TEN

As Chris and Uchechi made their way to the Widener Library, on their regular weekday ritual of visiting the home of the oldest library system in the United States and largest academic research material in the world, Uchechi watched his now famous university colleague, gingerly making his way up the steps to the magnificent edifice built by Eleanor Widener in memory of her late son and Harvard alum, Harry Widener.

Harvard had kept up its perfect start to the season with its win away at Amherst, and whilst it wasn't the nine-goal romp of Cornell or anything close to it, Chris remained the otherworldly force that had been since the start of the campaign.

Amherst came ready to play, and the downpour that turned the field of play into a muddy aberration, seemed to help their cause. John Adams, the Harvard goalkeeper, was apparently called into action a lot more than in the previous two games, but Harvard had their great core to thank for keeping control of the midfield: Billy Ward, Tony Davies and Emmanuel Boye. Ward and Davies were as important to the team as the

Igbo prodigy from Owerri and had garnered almost as much praise.

"How's the leg today?" Uchechi asked, as they got to the top of the steps leading to the entrance of the great library. He had first seen the limp when they met up the previous day on Monday, their first meeting since the Amherst game at the weekend that Uchechi hadn't gone with to…

"It's seemed to get better since yesterday, but not by much, as I'm sure you've noticed." That last part of Chris' answer followed by a laugh that was joined by Uchechi.

"I could see you were trying to hide the limp from the prying eyes of your fans, but I know you too well." Uchechi said laughing.

"I'm not just hiding it from our supporters, as they are on such a high and I want to keep their hope and enthusiasm high for the next game, but also from anyone else who might be watching. Scouting your opponents is as important to any gameplan as anything and we wouldn't want to alert our opponents that I might not be 100%."
"That makes sense. Didn't really think of that." Uchechi said as they made through the

main doors. He looked up as the doors opened, at the painting of the man who the library was built in memoriam of. Whenever he walked into the library and looked up at the face of Harry Widener, he felt pity that the life of the young-looking face in the painting was prematurely taken away in that well known tragedy in 1912, the sinking of the Titanic. The tragic sight also always made him remember to promise himself to never be caught either dead or alive on the onboard ships of any kind…

As they walked through the library, there were nods and smiles in their direction from staff and students. It was a phenomenon that Uchechi had seen build from the back end of their freshman year, when Chris' on field heroics had begun to get notoriety, but which had now blossomed into a full-fledged fandom, not just from students and staff, but also from the families that lived in and around the Cambridge area, as word of his most recent exploits enhanced a legendary story from the previous week.

The Amherst game had seen Chris score all four goals for Harvard in yet another starring turn in a great all round team performance, in which for the first time that season, their opponents had refused to capitulate in the face of the overwhelming talent of the Harvard Crimson. The game had eventually ended 4-2 in Harvard's favor after the go-ahead goal by Chris, finally succeeding in subduing their opponents and its home crowd. The only downside to the Harvard Crimson victory was the injury Chris had picked up during the game.

As they eventually settled into their seats to begin their one-hour session of study and research, Uchechi's eyes caught the sight of a beautiful animal skin coat worn by a girl studying in another part of the room.

"A rich girl." He thought to himself at first, admiring the beauty and rich look of the coat. He was very much aware that the richest and most prestigious families in America sent their children to Harvard to study, including of course, the current President of the United States and the late alum whose memory the building they were studying in. Some he knew, but for the most part, those from such families, blended in with the rest of the Harvard Yard crowd.

But, as Uchechi removed his gaze from the lady in question, he realized that he had found what had been thinking about since he had heard of his tribesman's latest exploits on the football pitch. A nickname befitting the man.

Back home, he hadn't known Chris on as close a personal level as he now did, and Chris, while famous in the town of Owerri, was very much a young lad, only a just little older than he was, and so never really stayed long enough in the town for his popularity to really cement itself enough in the psyche of the sports loving populace, to warrant a well-known nickname.

Uchechi was extremely proud of his friend's exploits on the field and had been thinking of ways to hail him in their own way whenever they were around each other, and looking again at the beautiful coat of the girl, he wondered why hadn't thought of it before. Agu. I've been away from home too long he mused to himself.

Whilst most of the world had the Lion as the de-facto King of the Jungle with its image, sound and likeness being used as the representation of power, strength and majesty, the Igbo people greatly admired the Leopard.

The typical Igbo man and woman are very intelligent, exceptionally adaptable to changing conditions, environment and circumstance. They can thrive as an individual, or as part of a community, are independent minded and are trailblazers wherever they might find themselves, and just might be the most commercially successful people to be found anywhere in the world. In fact, a common saying amongst the Igbo is that "If you travel to anywhere on this planet and you didn't find and Igbo man or woman, you can leave the place, as there is no money to be made there."

Most of those qualities espoused by the Igbo, of adaptability, exceptionalism and tenacity are the very qualities of a Leopard or as it is called in Igbo language, Agu, which lived alongside the Igbo at their present location, from time immemorial. The Igbo recognized that the Lion was the stronger animal, as confirmed by the Igbo proverb, Odum n'egbu Agu, meaning that the Lion will kill the Leopard, but admired the behavioral tendencies of the Leopard, which tended to mirror the qualities they espoused for themselves.

Hence, the greatest or bravest warriors in the land were titled Ogbuagu, "Killer of Leopards", in deference to the tenacity of

the animal that had to be hunted ferociously when found anywhere close to the village settlements.
As Uchechi and Chris left the library to head over to Eliot house to have lunch at Chris' residence, a practice of having lunch at either of their houses of residence, which they alternated amongst themselves once the period of study was done, Uchechi called out to his friend and fellow Igbo man, "Agu!"

"What brought about this hailing?" Chris asked laughing. "Is it because it's my turn to buy lunch? I'm not buying any extras today, just so you know!"

"Stop pretending." Uchechi replied laughing. "You know there can only be one reason where such a title can be used."

"Ha-ha. I haven't seen any Leopards anywhere. Have you?

"Yes, I have." Uchechi replied smiling. "It's seemed to have followed us all the way from home, and no one in the Northeast region of the United States seems to have any idea on how to slay it. I've decided it's time we identify this ferocious adversary to any challengers of Harvard's supremacy.

I'm calling this particular one, the Leopard of Eliot House."

"Hear, hear." Chris replied, laughing. "Long may he reign. Now let's get some lunch. I don't know about you, but I'm starving."

"Amen to that" Uchechi replied with a laugh, and then they strolled off towards Eliot as fast as Chris' injured leg would allow…

•

Chris didn't make it for that game against Williams, the leg injury he sustained in the previous game, proving too painful to overcome on such a short turnaround. Try as he did to do everything to regain a level of competitiveness, he just couldn't move that leg without pain, and the decision was eventually made to rule him out for that game, in the hopes that he might regain fitness for the next game to Dartmouth.

It wouldn't be the first game he would miss that season due to injury, but even more of annoying for Chris was the fact that it would also lead to the Harvard Crimson's first loss of the season, in an upset loss to Williams University.

He came back for the game against Dartmouth, a hard fought 2-1 come-from-behind victory for the Crimson, having missed a second game, against Columbia, albeit a four-goal victory against their fellow Ivy League school.

Chris' equalizer in that tense Dartmouth game, was as significant in the history books as it was in the game, with it equaling the single season tally for goals for the Harvard soccer team, at fifteen.

He was still not at a hundred percent fitness for that game, but had recovered enough to make the team, and play the pivotal role he played to get that result for his team and the raucous home crowd of his fellow Harvard students, who had come to see his phenomenal talent on display and cheer the Crimson to victory.

The Leopard of Eliot House would smash the Harvard goal scoring record for a single season in the next game with his sixteenth and seventeenth goals, and also tied the Ivy league record of goals scored in a new single season with his eighth goal.

This game was away to another Ivy league team, University of Pennsylvania or Penn as they were called. The team travelled to Philadelphia to meet their illustrious adversaries.
The season schedule was arranged in such a fashion as to provide a mixture of games, with some against Ivy league schools, and other games with nearby universities. Obviously, with Harvard being the original Ivy league institution in the United States, they loved to win that tournament and have bragging rights over the rest of their illustrious fellow campaigners.

Chris' decision to continue play while still not fully recovered from his earlier leg injury would eventually catch up to him in the city of brotherly love, as he limped off the field after he had scored his record-breaking goals, with this one looking like it would need an extended time of recovery on the sideline.

Chris wouldn't score another goal that season as the injuries piled up for him, but it didn't matter, as his first season with the Crimson became one not just for the record books, but also a source for the most un-ending story telling by Harvard Yard of the incredible talents of the sophomore from Nigeria.

He would be named to the All-Ivy first team, along with two of his teammates, Billy Ward and Tony Davies, reward for a phenomenal season for the Crimson in which they won the 1961 Ivy league championship.

It had been an extraordinary debut campaign for Chris, and a harbinger of great things to come…

CHAPTER ELEVEN

Uchechi stepped off the train and onto the platform of the station that still pleasantly surprised him with its size and magnificence, even though it wasn't the first time he had come through it. He moved quickly with the crowd as it emerged from depths of the station where the platforms were located, and up towards the main concourse.

Grand Central Terminal, the world's largest train terminal was as opulent as Uchechi had remembered when he had come over to see Emeka, his childhood friend now turned Columbia undergrad, in February on invitation to watch, along with thousands of others at the big screen in the terminal, John Glen become the first American astronaut to orbit the Earth.

The United States had fallen behind the Soviet Union in the space race at the time, and after a series of failures and postponements, America had held its collective breath for the Friendship 7 mission on February 20th, 1962. Emeka, who had been unable to come over to Cambridge last year when his university soccer team played Harvard due to illness, was only too pleased to get Uchechi to come over to New York to make up for it, and they couldn't have chosen a more incredible time to see each other for the first time since they had left their hometown of Owerri for America, two years earlier.

It had been an odd day to make a journey in the week as students with it being a Tuesday, but the mission had been cleared to launch that day after prior launch dates had been aborted. As it was to be such a pivotal day in American history with the attention of the entire nation affixed on the Cape Canaveral launch site, Uchechi and Emeka had then decided such a momentous day would be a great day to mark their reunion. They had watched along with thousands, the 9.47 am launch for as long as they could see the spacecraft, before leaving to see as much of New York as was possible in a day…

Uchechi walked onto that concourse and paused momentarily in wonder, just as he had done the first time, he had seen it. The shafts of daylight that streamed through the magnificent cathedral-like windows fitted high above close to the ceiling, puncturing the gloomily lit concourse with tens of light-filled spears.

That phenomenon of light, along with the architecture of the building always induced a feeling of being in the presence of the Most-High God, in Uchechi. It was like he was inside a church where a Sunday service was about to commence.

He shook himself out of his spiritual daydream and made his way past the beautiful clock atop the Grand Central Terminal information booth, and then out towards the open air of the world's biggest city, with Emeka waiting just outside with an Egyptian cab driver Ahmad, whom Uchechi had met during his February visit. Emeka found it difficult and expensive, mostly the former, in finding cabs for journeys across the city, but had flagged down the Egyptian one night while hailing for a cab, and after finding out that they actually lived close to one another, Emeka would give him a heads-up whenever he had a planned taxi journey to make, and Ahmad would accommodate him accordingly.

"Chief!" Emeka shouted to him across the din of traffic, both human and vehicular, to alert his friend as to where he was waiting. "You got here right on time. We didn't have to wait more than a few minutes, right Ahmad?"

“Perfect timing, boss.” Replied the man from Ismailia, as he helped Uchechi put his luggage in the back. “You’re staying longer this time?”

“Yes, Ahmad. The last time I came here in February, we were in the middle of the semester, and so I couldn’t stay long. Now we are on summer holidays, I can stay much longer, and see more of New York.”

“He’s going to be here for a month.” Emeka said as they started their journey and made their way through Manhattan to Emeka’s residence hall in Harlem, and then turning to his childhood friend. “I’m going to show you a few places I’ve discovered since the last time you were here. You’re going to love it. Wish you had been able to come for your birthday, New York is always great for a party.”

“Yes, brother. It would have been great to celebrate here, but Boston has its share of great places too, and you know Chris and I share June 19th as our birthday, right? Our friends had something planned for us there, too.

“Yes, of course.” Emeka acknowledged. “How is our celebrity friend doing, by the way? His name seems to be reverberating across the Northeastern corner of the United States, and the Ivy League schools in particular. His exploits on the field last season, was legendary. Tell him we are all proud of him, when you go back. I don't even mind if he smashes six goals against my team. I tell everyone I've known him for years, and immediately become a celebrity by association!"

They both laughed, and Uchechi said, "You can tell him yourself when you see him. He said to tell you that he's expecting you to show up in Cambridge, so we can spoil you a little and show you the beauty of Boston. I won't be back here until you come down to the Yard."

"That's a promise, brother. I'll be there on October 1st to celebrate Independence Day with you guys."

"That would be perfect, Emeka. That way we can plan a party and introduce you to a lot of people. Now, that's an Independence Day celebration to look forward to."

With that, Uchechi sat back in the back of Ahmad's cab and enjoyed the sights and sounds of the late July warmth of New York.

Summer in New York was just like summer in Boston, when it seemed like everyone came out from winter hibernation, with ladies in scantily clad outfits, enjoying the appearance of the most cheerful season of the year. For young men everywhere, it was the best season to meet and admire girls. A time of parties and barbecues across the land.

"Hey Emeka." Uchechi called to his friend as a thought popped into his head, "How's the girlfriend search going? Any luck so far?"

"It's not been easy bro. It's a big city and I get to meet a lot of people, but I hardly ever really get to know them. You know what I mean? You meet people, but not always people you want to get into a meaningful relationship with. The girls are absolutely beautiful, but I'm yet to meet one like the girl you described to me, Mary, wasn't it? You're lucky to have found such a great girl for yourself. Of course, it helps that you are able to meet and go to class with girls at Harvard. Unlike the Harvard and Radcliffe relationship in Cambridge, we would be so lucky to have such an understanding with Barnard College, Columbia University's female undergrad affiliate."

"I feel for your brother. We are so lucky to have female companionship at Harvard, albeit only in class. We still aren't allowed to cohabitate yet. But, thanks to the merging of the academic and other activities there are plenty of opportunities to mingle and socialize, whether in Harvard Yard or outside. Any discussions on that front for Columbia?"

"Nothing on the horizon, in this year of our Lord, 1962." Replied Emeka. "Not inclusive schooling and definitely not cohabitation. I fear that if it is going to happen, it would be long after I'd have left this university."

"Don't think much about it, brother." Uchechi said, noting the slightly wistful note in his friend's voice. "Maybe that's why fate has brought us again together again this week." He continued, with a laugh, "It will be the old one-two punch of Uchechi and Emeka, taking on the world of possibilities again."

"You mean the one-two punch team of Emeka…and Uchechi? Would that be the one you are referring to? Emeka replied laughing. "If that is the team you are referring to, then yes, New York has no chance."

They both got out of the cab laughing, as they had arrived at Emeka's Columbia University residence hall, John Jay, located in Harlem. Emeka took him round to introduce him to his friends in the building, which gave them a chance to explore a few floors, including the very top of the fifteen-story building, the penthouse as it was named, all of which showed off the magnificent views on each side of architectural edifice.

They popped out for a meal in the afternoon, so Emeka could show Uchechi the local area. They walked into Emeka's favorite hangout spot. It turned out to be a well-known diner that quite a few Africans hung out in. Not that they served any dish from back home, it was owned by a Jewish couple, but seemed to be one that that drew Africans who lived in the area to it.

There were a few Nigerian students in there to grab some lunch, and Emeka introduced them all to Uchechi, sparking exchanges of news and happenings concerning home and the diaspora, especially those in New York.

"Have you guys heard about the title fight between World Middleweight Champion Gene Fullmer and Dick Tiger in October?"

Asked Dele, a New York University student of Yoruba extinction from Ibadan, Nigeria. Dick Tiger was an Igbo man, real name Richard Ihetu, just like Uchechi and Emeka, and had cut a swarth through the middleweight ranks since his arrival in the United States a few years earlier. He was a hero throughout Igboland and Nigeria, the very first person of Igbo origin to attain his level of success in the sport of Boxing. He had won the Commonwealth Middleweight Boxing belt just 2 years prior and was now in line for a World Championship shot for the very first time.

“He’s won his last seven fights.” Uchechi replied “He looks like the most impressive fighter in the world this year, and I think he has a real chance to win it, if he performs like he’s being doing for a while now. Where’s the fight going to be held at?”

“San Francisco, across the country on the West Coast.” Emeka replied wistfully “It would have been great to go there in October and watch that fight live. I watched his fight against Henry Hank in March, and he was magnificent. I think he’s the best fighter in the world at the moment.”

“Did you watch his fight against William Pickett last December?” asked Jerry, a Liberian who had moved back to the United States from the West African country, in a move reversing the one made by his great-grandparents about 150 years earlier. “That was a great fight by him, but there was another young man introduced there that night, and who I think is going to be great. I’ve seen him fight, and he looks really good. I think his name is Cassius Clay.”

“Oh, I’ve heard of him.” Dele said. “He’s still up and coming, but right now, Dick Tiger is the best fighter in the world…or will be once he beats Gene Fullmer.”

“It would be great, if we were able to make it to San Francisco.” Uchechi said. “I bet the atmosphere will be magnificent.”

“Well, we’ve got 3 months to come up with a plan.” Emeka said. “If we come up with a viable plan, I’ll let you know on time, and maybe you can join us from Boston.”

They finished up their meal, and after exchanging goodbyes, made their way back to Emeka’s room at John Jay, so that they could plan their evening.

“There’s this place I discovered in Greenwich Village. It has a lot of great jazz musicians who go and perform there virtually every night. I’ve been there just one time a couple of weeks ago but haven’t been back. The music is great, and I know you’ll love it. Would you want to swing by there, tonight?”

“Absolutely.” Uchechi replied smiling, “My first club scene in New York. What’s not to like? Maybe, we might even get a girl for you!”

“Don’t get my hopes up like that, brother.” Emeka said laughing. “But yes, that would be very welcome. Let’s see what happens tonight.”

They spent the next few hours catching up on all matters concerning their families back home, friends and neighbors, as well as their various experiences in their respective campuses on matters of race, course difficulty, adaptation and of course their respective relationships with the opposite sex, or as in Emeka’s case with much hilarity, the lack of one. They then decided to catch a bit of rest in order so as to be fresh for their late evening sojourn at Emeka’s new favorite jazz club.

•

Ahmad's cab steadily made its way through Manhattan's evening traffic with his fellow Africans seated in the back, dressed in their proverbial Sunday best. The car windows had been lowered and the cool evening breeze washed through the car, keeping the temperature just about perfect for the midsummer night.

Everything seemed different in New York, like everyone was in a hurry to get to wherever it was that they desired to be but resigned to the fact that they could get there only as fast as the city traffic would let them. This led to a certain aggression in personality that seemed to define much of the great city's population to Uche's naked eye, especially as he had spent the majority of his life first in Owerri, and then in the Harvard confines of Cambridge.

Uchechi didn't mind the seeming "New York state of mind". He had just put it down to another aspect of the world that was to be learned about and added to his ever-growing world perspective of places, peoples and their environment.

"We're here." Emeka announced, as the cab pulled up to the entrance to the Village Vanguard, the former speakeasy on Seventh Street South in Greenwich. They paid Ahmad and hopped out of the car, thanking him as he drove away.

The interior of the club had the shape of a triangle, probably the reason it had been named The Golden Triangle during its short run prior to being obtained by Max Gordon, the owner of Emeka's newly discovered jazz club.

As the made their way to the table, Uchechi looked towards the stage where a quartet was playing music that seemed to make the ground he trod on, as soft as freshly fallen snow. There were four Black men, African-Americans he thought, performing a beautiful jazz number, so beautiful it was that he didn't notice that they had been seated right next to a couple of stunning African American girls, to be truthful, he hadn't realized how they had gotten to the table, so engrossed was he in the music coming from the jazz quartet on the stage. Well, he hadn't noticed, but Emeka surely had…

“Hi ladies” Emeka called to them “Seems like we’ve got some great music tonight”. This, less than a minute after they had sat down, a time that Uchechi felt was too soon to try chatting up the girls, but he was proved wrong as the girl closest to them replied.

“Yeah. It’s John Coltrane and his band playing their brand-new album. You know who he is? You’re not a regular on the jazz scene, are you?”. This said while shifting her gaze between the two of them. Uchechi couldn’t be sure if the look in her eye was one of derision for not knowing who John Coltrane was, and noticing Emeka’s slight hesitation, wondered if Emeka was thinking the same thing…

“I’m a visitor to New York, just come over from Boston” He replied. “I’m studying in Harvard and came to catch up with my friend here, and we thought we’d come here tonight.”

“Yeah. I’ve only ever been here once myself, and I’m still new to the jazz scene.” Emeka said, “So yes, you’re right, we’re both new to jazz, but we like it. By the way, my name’s Emeka and this is my friend Uchechi.”

“That’s cool, brother.” My name is Mary, and this is my friend Sarah.” This said as she looked to her friend, who had turned her attention from the band to the discussions between her friend and the strangers from the next table.

“You two are African, right?” Sarah asked.

“Yes, we are.” Emeka replied. “Specifically of Igbo origin from Nigeria.”

“Are you both studying here?” Mary asked.

“Yes, we are.” I’m studying at Columbia, while he’s over in New England, studying at Harvard as he said.”

“That’s really cool, guys.” Sarah said. “Nice to meet you. We’re both studying at New York University. Mary and I come down here any chance we get.”

“Yeah, call us the quintessential jazz lovers.” Mary said, as they all started laughing. Sarah here, was even named after the great jazz singer, Sarah Vaughan, so yeah, she was born to love jazz.”

They paused the conversation as the audience in the jazz club burst into applause, as the band finished the number they had been playing.

“What was the name of the jazz number they just finished playing?” Uchechi asked the girls. “I really enjoyed it.”

“It’s called Tunji.” Sarah replied. I’ve got the album at home, but jazz is always great to listen to live, as there will always be improvisations, which makes the music even more magical.”

“It’s funny that you would like that one.” Mary said, as they all ordered a fresh round of drinks. “It’s actually dedicated to another Nigerian musician, who’s known in jazz circles too. His name is Michael Babatunde Olatunji, a great drummer.”

“He’s a great guy too.” Added Sarah. “He actually graduated from our university years ago, and has been involved in the Civil Rights Movement, right from the early days, while he was still at Morehouse College, down south in Georgia.”
“He’s pretty much an icon on the music scene, here in New York.” Mary added. “I’m sure you’ll get to meet him at some

point if you hang around New York long enough."

"So, will you be staying for much longer in New York?" Sarah asked Uchechi.

"Only for a week. Just got in earlier today, so it's up to Emeka to show me the best of what New York has to offer."

"So where are you planning on taking him?" Sarah asked.

"I'll play it by ear." Emeka replied. "It's more of a catch-up visit for us. We grew up together back in Owerri, Nigeria. So, we'll just have fun and go to wherever catches our eye. How about you two? Where do you go for fun in this town? I assume you grew up here, right?"

"I did." Mary replied. "I live here with my boyfriend, and only just moved out of my parents' place in Harlem. But Sarah, whom I met when we both started at NYU, actually didn't grow up here."

"Yeah. I grew up in New Jersey but was actually born in Virginia before my parents decided to move north, like a lot of other African American families from down south

at the time, and even still today. Racism is a lot more prevalent down south, not that it is so much better as you head north, but things can get pretty dangerous down that way, and my parents didn't want to put up with it anymore.
Do you two follow the Civil Rights movement here in America? And what's it been like for you over there in Boston? I've heard stories of that town…"

"I have noticed it a couple of times in Boston." Uchechi replied, "But, I've been lucky to have had a great couple take care of me when I first got there, and that greatly helped me settle in this country. Also, the Harvard community has been great at making sure we settled into the community. That and the fact that I have a few of my West African brothers studying at Harvard, has made things a lot less daunting."

"And yes." Emeka added. "We definitely follow the Civil Rights here. In fact, Nigeria only attained independence less than two years ago, and so we are acutely aware of what it can be like to be a secondary participant in the affairs of your own country. I'm certain that something will change soon, as long as we keep up the pressure on the State and Federal governments. It took decades of protest and pressure to force Great Britain to leave us to rule our own country."

"Hallelujah to that" exclaimed Sarah, to which a ripple of laughter cut through the solemn mood at the table. It wasn't a laughter of disbelief at the notion of things changing for the better in the US, but rather one of confidence in the purpose and success of the greatest movement for justice in United States history.

"As for what our plans for the week, are?" Sarah continued. "Well, we both love our music, which is actually why we go out together. So, we'll probably be looking to head out to some joint or the other."

"Actually, there is a show happening at The Village gate this week." Mary said. I think it's Nina Simone."

"It would be great to catch up with you two again." Emeka said. "That is of course, if you'll actually remember our names." This bringing laughter from the girls. "I'm certain you haven't heard those names before."

"No, we haven't." Sarah said still laughing. "But you two aren't the only ones with

unusual names. My middle name is actually Ada. A rare name to be found here in New York, or anywhere in the States I would think, but it was my grandma's name back in Virginia and my father say's I look just like she did, and there's quite a few women named Ada, in our old community.
So, relax. She continued with a smile. "You see, you're not the only ones with rare names around here. I'll be sure be sure to remember your names when we meet again."

"Are you a first-born girl in your family?" Uchechi asked suddenly, having quickly exchanged a glance with Emeka.

"Yes, I am. Why?"

"It's just that, it's a name and title given to first-born daughters in Igboland." Emeka answered. "Fancy that, we hear that name with a sister, who's also a first-born daughter, over here in America. We are pleasantly surprised at the coincidence."

"You do know, now that you say that, back during the days of slavery, a lot of Igbo slaves came through Virginia." Sarah said. "Now I know why when you called the name of your people, I thought I'd heard that name before."

"Hey." Uchechi exclaimed with a smile, eliciting another round of laughter out of the seated group. "This night is just getting better and better. Who knew we would find a long-lost sister, right in the heart of New York?"

"Alright then." Mary said with a smile. "Will definitely be great catching up again with you two. I think the show is on Thursday at The Village Gate. Will you two be able to make it there?"

"How does 7pm on Thursday, sound?" Emeka asked.

"We'll be there." Sarah replied, and with that they settled down, continuing to savor the musical genius of John Coltrane and his great quartet…

•

They met up again as planned at The Village Gate, to enjoy the greatness of Nina Simone as she performed the songs from her album, Nina at the Village Gate. The even met Michael Babatunde Olatunji, who had also

written a track on the album called "Zungo", performed to such a perfection by the great lady herself, in such unmistakable Yoruba lyrical and rhythmical style, that it took all the self-restraint by Uchechi to not get up and do a dance.
It was a truly magical night, for whilst Mary brought her boyfriend, Sarah turned out not to have one, and had struck up a good rapport with Emeka, the only other person not in a relationship in their party, in such a fashion that, by the time Uchechi had left New York, the two had begun planning dates to go on by themselves, to the absolute delight of Uchechi.

It was to be the last time he would visit New York, but as he watched the landscape as the train sped to Boston, he wasn't to know that or particularly care. It was a trip he would treasure and remember for the rest of his life.

CHAPTER TWELVE

The 1962-63 academic session seemed to go by rather quickly, or maybe they all realized how close they were to finishing their first degree at Harvard, and there was no room for any letdown in their dedication to making the very best of the opportunity their scholarships had provided them.

Their penultimate year hadn't started any different from the previous one. Chris proceeded to continue his assault on the Ivy League soccer record books with the same vigor and single-minded dedication as his first season. He had healed up from the injuries that had disrupted his availability in the past and returned with the added experience from playing against the Crimson's Ivy league opponents.

From his three-goal season debut against Tufts, and then the Ivy league first game against Cornell, he didn't let up. Not even when playing against childhood friends, as would happen in certain games (the exploits of Chris in his debut season had opened all eyes to the athletic potential of African students), and as was to become a more regular phenomenon throughout that season.

Everyone thought that opposing coaches and their defenses, would have made special preparations for “the leopard” coming into the season, having generally had sideline seats to his mesmerizing displays game after game, but it didn’t seem to matter what formations the coaches and players that were on the opposing side came to the field with, they only ever seemed to push him to even higher levels of performance.

Chris’s football exploits and responsibilities for Harvard, as well as their realization that they were at a crucial tenure in their academic scholarship, meant that any plans to go to Candlestick Park in San Francisco to watch Dick Tiger fight Gene Fullmer for the WBA Middleweight belt were scrapped.

It so happened that the greatest fight promoter in Boston and New England history, Sam Silverman, gave a closed-circuit television event of the live title fight happening on the other side of the country, having secured the rights for it. This news was greeted with much celebration by the Nigerian contingent of the Harvard student body, and even more by Chris and Uchechi, as it would give them the opportunity to see their fellow Igbo man perform in his glorious quest.

They quickly contacted Emeka in New York, of the once in a lifetime opportunity to see the fight, and also to fulfill his promise to come down to Boston and meet with them. The season schedule had the Harvard Crimson going off to New York to play Columbia University at Baker field on October 20th, 3 days before the Dick Tiger Vs Fullmer world title fight.

Unlike the game from the year before, the game was competitive with Chris scoring two goals in a 4-2 victory with Emeka in attendance, quietly cheering his longtime friend with pride, but furtive enough as to not attract the attention of his fellow Columbia mates.

Emeka had actually brought Sarah over to the game, her first time watching a soccer game, as Americans referred to it, and instantly became a fan of Chris' skill and prowess, especially as they were to journey back with him on a train to Boston, to stay a few days and catch the title fight in Boston.

They spent most of the train journey catching up on everything they could remember, Emeka and Chris, as well as introducing his new girlfriend Sarah, whom Chris had been briefed about by Uchechi, but in seeing her in the flesh, could see why Uchechi had raved about her, and mentally doffed a hat to his friend on his choice.

Uchechi had stayed back in Boston to make sure that Emeka and Sarah would have adequate accommodation for their stay. At first, it was mooted that Emeka stay with Uchechi, whilst Sarah sleepover at Mary's room in the Radcliffe quadrangle, but they all didn't think it would be good keeping the couple away from each other, especially as they were staying over in Boston for a few days.

Eventually, a small motel was found that would be both affordable and convenient for the couple, booked and paid for by the time their train had arrived at South Station. They all enjoyed the sights of Boston on the Sunday, Chris, Uchechi, Mary, Kofi alongside the visiting couple to the delight of Sarah, and they were welcomed and introduced to the Harvard student community at the Yard the following day on Monday, with everything running to plan for the visit.

Of course, as is customary in the world, things in this life never go as exactly as is planned, as it so happened that Monday,

October 22nd, was also the day that President Kennedy announced to a shocked nation, about a situation down in Cuba amounting to a blockade, in what would become to be known as the Cuban Missile Crisis.

They all huddled together alongside what seemed like the entire population of Harvard Yard, wondering if the much-ballyhooed nuclear conflict that had been predicted for years, ever since the creation of the atomic bomb, between the United States and the Soviet Union, was finally upon the world.

It served to dampen their enthusiasm for the future in the short term, but only temporarily, as the day of the fight rolled in with nary a plume of a mushroom cloud in sight, they prepared to get good seats to watch the relay of sporting spectacle at the Boston Arena.

Uchechi had never been to a fight, and neither did any of the rest of the group; Chris, Kofi, Mary, Emeka and Sarah. It was also the first time that they had seen the fighters on anything other than newspaper photos and posters, and while Dick Tiger was in as perfect a condition as a human being could be, with body definition that shone from the screen, and Gene Fullmer looked like the fearsome fighter whose reputation had always preceded him since his fights with the then aging Sugar Ray Robinson, it looked to Uchechi who knew a thing or two about weight classes, that Fullmer had to be a bigger fighter than his tribesman, Richard Ihetu aka Dick Tiger.

Regardless, once the opening bell had been rung, Dick Tiger took the fight to the world champion, constantly moving forward and forcing Fullmer backwards, taking punches whilst doing so but steadfastly giving a lot more punishment, a whole lot more.

It was always said that, to beat a champion, especially in boxing, you had to literally wrest the title at of his grasp, and it would appear that Richard Ihetu knew that as well. Or maybe, it was just the way a man who had lost the first four fights to start his career in a foreign land, mismanaged as he was, had learnt to forge ahead and overcome the odds on his way to greatness.

Uchechi and his band of fellow Dick Tiger fans cheered every punch thrown and every body blow recovered from, on that glorious night of fifteen rounds of some of the highest quality of boxing and human endurance, ever seen by the human eye.

Once the fight drew to a close, with a greeting of respect between the two warriors, two men from Fullmer's corner who had come to the center of the ring to meet the now fatigued warriors where they stood, no longer a danger to one another, and tapped Dick Tiger on the back and shoulder as he turned away towards his corner, an acknowledgement and appreciation for what he had accomplished long before the judges' scorecards were revealed, signaling to the eyes of all present and watching what they could already tell, that a new world middleweight champion was about to be crowned.

As Dick Tiger was carried on shoulders around the ring in the aftermath of the judges' decision with cheers from the watching crowd, Uchechi and his friends made their way out of the arena, celebrating loudly as they did, on their way to the nearest place they could order a drink from.

For those who had been lucky to witness it, it had been a welcome distraction from the issue hanging over the world at that time, something Uchechi only remembered as he waved to Emeka and Sarah, as they made their way back to New York from South Station.

That whole week felt surreal with everyone quietly wondering about their mortality; including the young, a rarity if there was ever one. People went on panic buying sprees, anticipating food shortages should the disagreements between the United States and the Soviet Union degenerate into conflict, whilst others wondered what packing food and supplies would really accomplish, if nuclear conflict was the end result of the crisis.

Thankfully, after a week, calmer heads seemed to win out as the Soviet Union withdrew their missiles from Cuba, the root cause of the crisis, whilst the United States ended their blockade of the Caribbean Island country, as well as other requested conditions for peace.

That Christmas, Uchechi took Mary to go visit Clifford and Catherine in Boston. He had always maintained the great relationship that they had had from his first day in Boston, one that he appreciated and treasured.
They were especially happy to see him and Mary together, they had known about her for a while, and took the time over dinner getting to know her, her family and plans for

the future, as any parent would when the future wellbeing of their child was involved. Uchechi's parents might have been thousands of miles away, on another continent a world away from the New England surroundings their son found himself in, but they needn't have worried for the wellbeing of their first-born son, as the Clarke's had basically adopted Uchechi as their own, and there was no safer place for him outside of his ancestral homeland, in all of the world.

They welcomed in 1963 together as one, toasting to an even better year ahead, whilst Uchechi waited for the morning to break, so that he could get his parents on the phone, talk and pray with them, and catch up with his brothers and sister in yet another year.

1963, as it would turn out, wasn't just a good year, but as it would gradually reveal itself to be, it was a great year. Not just for the people living in God's own country, but as it would turn out a great year for the country itself and African Americans in particular, as the nation slowly but surely, began the process of moving in the direction of shedding its ugly history concerning race.

There had been numerous protests over the last few years to go along with segregation breaking milestones; from the bill signed into law by President Harry Truman in 1948, de-segregating the military, to the Brown Vs the Board of Education Supreme Court judgement forcing the de-segregation of schools in 1954, The murder of Emmitt Till in 1955 via lynching and Rosa Parks refusing to leave her bus seat, all the way down to the Freedom Riders of 1961.

All these had helped inch the needle of justice in the direction of equity and justice, but there were still major hurdles faced by African Americans, as the calendar of 1963 began its steady progress through the months, until the month of April arrived, and with it a headwind of activity in the city of Birmingham, Alabama in the country's deep South.

Martin Luther King Jnr and the Southern Christian Leadership Conference (SCLC) had decided to launch a multi-faceted protest campaign against the city of Birmingham's system of racial segregation, with a series of boycotts and marches designed to bring attention to injustices and unequal treatment meted out to the African American community.

The initial campaign didn't have much of an effect if any, on the resolve of the city's leadership to either acknowledge that there was an issue, or even meet the protesters for some type of dialogue. This forced MLK and the other protest organizers to up the ante, which resulted in young people of school going age being allowed to join the protests, whereupon which the city and its law enforcement arm made a critical mistake, which was to turn the country's attitude to Civil Rights in the course of a few days and weeks.

The images beamed around the country of water cannons being deployed on the children, along with being bitten by vicious police dogs, caused so much outrage in the nation, and flipped the opinion of Americans who had been largely indifferent on the issue of Civil Rights to a largely engaged and furious country at the scenes being beamed into their homes via their television sets of the barbaric acts by white law enforcement on defenseless and innocent African Americans.

In Cambridge Massachusetts, Harvard students began gathering at the Cambridge Common in anger and solidarity at what they had just witnessed days earlier.

Uchechi, Chris, Kofi, Mary Dawn, Jane, Carla, Ann and Carl were joined by hundreds of students as they walked in hand in hand, together as one regardless of race, religion or gender, unified by the horrors they had witnessed on TV and read about in just about every newspaper that could be found and the desire to push for a much-needed change.

As they marched down the road, they were quickly joined by students from other institutions in the Boston area, before joining, at first apprehensively, and then slowly and respectfully, a large gathering of African Americans including Carl's girlfriend Angie, whom he left the group to go and stand next to, right along with all the students of Harvard, Radcliffe, M.I.T and Boston University.

It would be the first time many of the students of these institutions would be involved, not just with the Civil Rights movement that was emerging throughout the country, but also, and especially with the students of Harvard, the first time they would really be interacting with the larger Boston community that didn't necessarily look like themselves.

Thus, in the midst of the savagery of the Birmingham, Alabama authorities, as is sometimes the case with harbingers of evil and tyranny, had unwittingly given birth to something that they had not foreseen or wished to see; the beginning of the inclusive nature of the Civil Rights movement across race, religion and gender, giving the movement the popular backing and awareness, it had wanted but been unable to actualize.

This inclusive nature would carry over into the formerly unheralded, but now pivotal March on Washington DC, which would take place in August that year in the nation's capital, the eyes and ears of the world now keenly following the events of the day.

Uchechi, his friends, along with a big contingent of Harvard students, made the trip to participate in what would turn out to be the most famous, and pivotal of Civil Rights marches to take place in the history of the United States. About a quarter of the estimated quarter of a million people that came to Washington DC that day weren't black, solidifying the broad appeal and reach of the issue of the day.

Uchechi, along with Emeka who had also made the trip form New York, along with Sarah, Mary and her boyfriend, noticed the presence of Michael Babatunde Olatunji, the Yoruba percussionist extraordinaire, or rather they heard him, pacing the crowd with the soothing and yet rallying nature of his beat. It was just one of the things that made that march so memorable. Then of course that speech… The “I have a dream” speech from Dr King that will resonate for time immemorial, both for those fortunate enough to hear it in person that day, and for the millions that would seek to tap into its unfading greatness in the decades to come.

Civil Rights was not the only issue that was holding the attention of the United States in 1963 as Uchechi and his friends entered into their final year of their bachelor’s degree. The Vietnam War was gradually entering into the peripheral vision for the American public.

As was the custom in the politically savvy institution that was Harvard, learning home to Presidents, Governors and Senators too numerous to mention, you never quite knew what important future personality you were addressing when you arrived at Harvard Yard, or what important present day politician's scion you would be making an impression on.

As it was that October day, it was Madame Ngo Dinh Nhu, the de facto first lady of South Vietnam, the President was unmarried, where the activities of the husband's regime had preceded her, precipitating a hostile reception for her speech at the Harvard Law forum, on the closing leg of what she had hoped to be public relations mission to improve the image of the regime of her husband, who whilst not President was considered to largely run the fledgling South Asian country, and his brother the bachelor President.

The trip was largely considered a disaster, and it would appear that those forces both within and outside South Vietnam had enough, and in brutal circumstances, just as had befallen their eldest brother for his part in a rebellion against the French colonial government years earlier, both her husband and his brother were killed on the 2nd of November, whilst she was still in the United States.

It was a foreboding of a terrible month to come in Harvard history.

Friday, the 22nd of November 1963, felt like any other Friday when the daylight broke. The final day of the work/study week leading into the weekend, with everyone making plans as to what they wanted to do with the free time on offer. Travel, parties or just plain rest.

Chris and the Crimson soccer team had travelled to New Haven to play Yale that afternoon, and so there wasn't any game on at the field for Uchechi and Kofi to watch, and so the two of them along with Mary, Ann(whom had been going out with Kofi for a while) and Chris, planned to go out into the Boston area to meet up with Angie, who was trying to introduce them to a new small diner in Boston that served up Southern Fried food, a particular favorite of she and Carl.

Uchechi and Kofi went out towards the Radcliffe quadrangle to meet up with Mary and Ann, and then head down to the Harvard station to begin the journey to Boston and catch up with Carl who had already gone ahead to meet Angie.

"He's been shot!" was the shout that signaled the first indication of the terrible deed that had been done down in Dallas,

Texas just after midday. First, there had been confusion, who was it that had been shot? Then, as the explanation began to filter through around Harvard Yard, followed almost immediately by the horrible and seemingly inevitable update, people began sobbing, not just in the Cambridge confines of Harvard, but all around the America and the world.

President John F. Kennedy, the Massachusetts scion who had graduated from Harvard just 23 years earlier, had been on a tour of the Southern parts of the United States when tragedy struck in Dallas at midday. An assassin had murdered, with long distance shots to the head and neck, one of the most loved American Presidents since the inception of the country in 1776.

It hit more deeply in New England, and especially in Harvard Yard. He hadn't just been the President; he was their President. A man who had taken the same steps in life that they were currently taking and had used those steps as part of his platform to the top. That was a charismatic man who seemed to always espouse the lofty ambitions that they had, and even though he was a quarter century older, it only underlined the sphere

of influence his leadership had on the institution.
Even more than that, he had always found the time to come back to his alma mater and spend time with the students of the day, who were making their way through the esteemed gauntlet of storied education. He was a flesh and bone reminder and inspiration on the possibilities of achievement in life after Harvard. He had only been present at the University on October 19th, to watch a football game. No one at that game knew that it was to be his final appearance at the storied institution.

The trip to meet up with Carl and Angie was cancelled, as the two girls were absolutely distraught over the horrible news, which Uchechi was sure Carl would expect, as news on the day's events made its way to him, where he and Angie were.

The assassination was a reminder that there was still a lot of work to be done to keep the nation together and moving in the right direction. The return from the trip to Washington DC for the March in August, had been euphoric with a semblance of great changc and hope for the future.

The progress of the Civil Rights movement, a movement that had benefitted from the contributions of the last three Presidents, Presidents Truman, Eisenhower and the now dead John F. Kennedy, now lay in state of uncertainty about the actions of the incoming President Lyndon B. Johnson, noting the exceptional hand of influence that JFK had in doing his part to help the movement along with his brother, the Attorney- General, Robert Kennedy.

They were not to worry, as the most sweeping changes to the uneven hand of segregation and injustice to minorities by use of landmark legislation, would be accomplished during the Presidential years of Lyndon Johnson.

Before those triumphs were actualized, the work of educating the masses about the unfairness and effects of segregation and discrimination by race on society, continued undeterred. Speakers on the subject, both for and against, made their way to Harvard, honoring invites of the various student activist bodies.

George Wallace, the pro-segregation Governor of Alabama came on an invite from the Young Democrats, with him being a popular member of the Democratic party, proclaiming that race relations in the segregated American South, were actually better than in the historically more racially liberal minded North, a continuation of his unwavering racist support for the continued relegation of African Americans to the lower rungs of society, to the dismay of protesting Harvard students. Even worse, he had managed to get a sizable number of students to attend his lecture.

Countering that narrative, James Baldwin, the acclaimed African American writer and Civil Rights advocate, delivered a lecture on the culture and history of African Americans, a counter argument to the ludicrous notion at the time, that Black people had no culture.

Malcolm X, the second most recognizable leader of the Civil Rights movement, and one with a slightly different approach to the achievement of the goal of equality for African Americans, who had just broken away from the Nation of Islam and its leader Elijah Mohammed, came to Harvard to talk of the need for African Americans to have control over their resources and community.

Uchechi had gone to that lecture, so enthralled was he by the speaking qualities of Dr King, that he had wanted to see Malcolm X after hearing that the man was no less gifted in his ability to motivate through speaking and ideas, a quality not lost on the Igbo son, whose people also put a premium on the effective ability to communicate ideas in the greatest possible way.

In a few years both icons, Dr King and Malcolm X, would lose their lives to the bullets of cowardly assassins, just as the other great orator of the decade, President Kennedy had been. A sad commentary on the temporary triumph of violence, over the greatest advocates of change and peace in that tumultuous, world changing decade.

This was the setting for Uchechi's final year at Harvard. So much happening at the same time, both at Harvard Yard and in the outer world, that there was nary an opportunity to stop and enjoy the significance of that last year, and there were plenty of significant events that had nothing to do with study or the volatility of the world around.

Uchechi and Mary made the trip to see her parents at their home just outside Boston, a trip that he had dreaded for the longest time. As much as he had known Mary all those years, he didn't know her parents, and in the prevailing climate of race relations and the Civil Rights movement in America, he had no way of knowing how they would feel about their white daughter marrying a stranger from the African continent…especially as they were planning on getting married, with her moving back to live with him in Nigeria.

Her parents were nice and polite, more her mother than her dad, but Uchechi understood that it would not be easy for parents to see their children live far away where it would be difficult to see them, something Uchechi could empathize with as his parent were desperate for his return after four long years away.

There and then, and totally unprompted, after she had broken their plans to her parents, he had promised that they would travel back to the United States as often as they could, and that it had not been set in stone that they would living permanently in Nigeria.

Her parents seemed to take the news well, even though Uchechi was under no illusions that there would be further discussions on the topic when he wasn't there, which would determine how well their plans could progress. He, however, knew Mary well enough, to know how she could be unwavering in any quest she was involved in, once she believed strongly in it.

He watched her father hold her just fractionally longer than he would, and knew he would take the news harder, as he knew of the enduring love between fathers and their first daughters, just as he was familiar of the similar connection between mothers and their first sons.

As they made their way back to Cambridge via train, Uchechi smiled. It had been a long adventure of discovery, personal growth and future opportunity in God's own country, but as he snatched a look at the beautiful girl beside him, he was totally convinced that the greatest prize he had won was not one he had come to America to find, but one that would be walking by his side for as long as God's mercies would allow them…

CHAPTER THIRTEEN

It had been a year and half since graduation from Harvard followed by their relocation to Nigeria, but it felt to Uchechi and Mary that they had spent less than half of that time in the West African country as their Peugeot sped along the road towards Uchechi's ancestral village of Atta, some 30 mins north of their residential town of Owerri.

Saying goodbye to Boston hadn't been easy. Whilst they both had exceptional grade point averages for their various degrees, confirming to themselves and their families that they had made the best possible use of the opportunity to attend the most prestigious university in the land, it was the goodbyes that were to be said to the families they had come to be a part of at Harvard Yard and the Radcliffe Quadrangle.

For Uchechi, it meant saying goodbye to Kofi, Carl and his girlfriend Angie, Mary's friends, as well as all the people at Harvard Yard that had made his four-year sojourn in New England, the success that it had turned out to be.

But of course, the hardest goodbye that had to be said was to the couple that had acted as

his surrogate parents in America, the first people who had made him welcome and given him shelter and a base to confidently go out in a strange, new land.
Catherine could barely hold back tears that afternoon at lunch, as Uchechi and Mary had come down to Boston for one last visit before they would get on their flight in the next few days. Clifford was quiet through most of the meal, which Uchechi understood as they sat across from one another on the table.
He would always remember the times spent with the couple and all they had done, a lot well outside the license they had, just making that extra effort to make sure he could integrate confidently into the new society he had been thrust into.

Uchechi and Mary, who had always liked the couple from the first time they had met, promised that they would be back to see them, whilst Catherine insisted that she and Clifford would be seeing off them off on their day of departure.

The goodbyes exchanged with Kofi were bittersweet, as while they were both excited about graduating with great scores, graduation also meant that they would be headed back to their respective countries;

Nigeria and Ghana, with a slim possibility that they might ever meet again, unless one of them had business or some other thing, that would necessitate travel to the other country. There were memories of their various shared experiences that would have to do until they met again.

Then, of course, there was the "home crew" for whom goodbyes weren't needed.

Chris, just as Emeka had done, had eventually settled with an African American girl named Shirley, and they along with Emeka and his girlfriend Sarah, would travel back to Owerri in 1964 after graduation for a short visit, to visit their respective families for the first time in four years, not just for the ecstatic welcome home from their parents, but also to introduce their girlfriends, both of whom they'd go on to marry.

Those weeks, short as they were, turned out to be perfect for Mary, whom Uchechi had introduced to his parents at the same period. She had found a few familiar faces to talk to whilst getting acclimatized to her new environment, even if was just for a while. For whilst, Shirley and Sarah would be returning to the United States with their future husbands, Mary would be staying in the heart of Igboland with Uchechi, as they attempted to build a life together East of the great Niger River.

After the introductions had been done, and Uchechi and his parents had got together for a private sit-down to discuss the day's event. With Uchechi being the first-born son, the next head of the family following his father, the subject of marriage was as important an issue as could be in the life of an Igbo family.

"Are you sure she is going to stay? What about your children? Will they be brought up to be proud Igbo men and women, or will they lose the identity of our family and our people, and become in essence, lost?"

These questions all had to be answered, and rightly so. Even then, a slow realization had begun to dawn on Igbo parents, just as they had started to embrace the prospect of travelling outside of their ancestral lands in ever-growing numbers, that the cultural identity of children born either outside of Nigeria or to foreign mothers was not as strong as it should normally be, and in some cases, scarily absent.

Henry and Akunna Chukwuka had no intention of letting that happen to the next generation of Chukwukas, and to their relief, in spite of whatever emotions that had brought together the couple now residing in their compound, neither did their son. He had explained to them that both he and Mary, had discussed the upbringing of their potential children and where they would live, and that they both had actually wanted to see if they could make a good living in Nigeria.

The prospect of having their son home, along with the potential to watch their grandchildren grow up, had calmed any fears Uchechi's parents had harbored, especially as they watched his friends make their way back to the United States after a few weeks.

Akunna Chukwuka began embracing the presence of her new daughter, Mary. She appreciated the courage it must have taken for her to leave her parents half a world away, in order to join Uchechi to stay in his.

Henry Chukwuka for his own part, was happy that both Uchechi and Mary intended to be legally married as soon as his and Akunna's consent to the marriage was obtained. He smiled quietly to himself later, thinking back to the growth in his son over the past four years, physically, emotionally and most importantly, mentally.

The two returned briefly to the United States for the wedding in the church Mary had grown up worshipping in. Chris and Shirley, Emeka and Sarah, Clifford and Catherine along with a host of invited guests, joined the new couple celebrate their nuptials just outside Boston. Uchechi's Uncle James came all the way from Los Angeles to represent Uchechi's side of the family.

They returned to Owerri after their honeymoon on the West Coast, where Mary took up a job as an economist for a local firm and Uchechi set up an engine repair company, and from these opportunities they managed to purchase some land and build a home not too far away from Uchechi's parents.

Mary gave birth to their first child on New Year's Eve in'65, making the celebrations of the coming year of 1966, doubly special. They named him Uzoma, meaning the way ahead would be good…

But as they arrived Atta that evening, joining the rest of the Chukwuka family, they had realized that 1966 was not looking as great as it did six months earlier. The dark clouds that they could see gathering in the horizon, were emblematic of the year in Nigeria…

•

The January 15th coup led by Major Kaduna Nzeogwu, Emmanuel Ifeajuna (the first Black African to win a Commonwealth Games Gold Medal, only 12 years earlier) and others, which led to the murders of the Prime Minister, Abubakar Tafawa Balewa, the Premiers of the Western and Northern Regions, Ladoke Akintola and Ahmadu Bello respectively, amongst others, would bring to a premature end, the First Republic of Nigeria. However, a dark narrative had begun to circulate and permeate the consciousness of the multi-ethnic Nigerian populace.

Whilst that coup was put down eventually by Igbo officers in the army Major-General Aguiyi Ironsi and Lt Col Emeka Ojukwu, the murders of thc most revered politicians from the other regions of the country except the east, which was majority Igbo, also the ethnic group that the majority of the recognized coup leaders came from, led to deep resentment from many non-Igbos, whatever the reason for the failure to execute the plan on politicians of Igbo origin in the country might have been.

That dark undercurrent of resentment would be forcefully be brought to the surface on July 29th 1966 in the form of a counter coup led by officers in the army of Northern extraction, just six months after the January coup, and unlike its predecessor successful, due to the brutal murders of Major- General Ironsi, who had taken over the helm of the country's affairs in the aftermath of the unsuccessful January coup, and his host, the brave Col Adekunle Fajuyi who had refused to allow his Commander-in Chief be brutalized whilst in his home and under his protection. His sense of responsibility and bravery would ultimately cost him his life alongside Ironsi, in reportedly brutal circumstances.

The killings didn't end there, as the Northern soldiers decided also that they would murder just about every officer of Igbo extraction in the army that they could lay their hands on, causing the lucky ones who survived the murderous blitz to flee back East, the only place they would be safe.

The Hausa/Fulani people in the north, seeing the balance of power shift towards army officers from their part of the country, as well as the murders of Igbo officers across the country, turned their attention on Igbo people living in the communities, deciding to exact revenge for the perceived murder of their beloved leaders six months earlier.

Igbo people have always been incredible traders and business entrepreneurs, best known, both inside and outside Nigeria, for their ability to quickly adapt to whatever environment they found themselves in and thrive. This meant that they, more than any other ethnic group in the country, could be found in virtually every area of Nigeria. This ability to thrive outside their own region, seeing and taking advantage of opportunities hitherto unseen by others, would turn out to be an unforeseen and unfortunate chink in their armor, used by the people who whilst from a different tribe and religion, they had considered neighbors and fellow countrymen and women for years.

The pogroms that followed by soldiers from the Northern region and Muslim mobs would eventually lead to the deaths of an estimated 30,000 Igbo people, whilst all the rest fled back to their home region, abandoning everything they had to escape the killings.

This was the scene that Uchechi and Mary had come back to when they arrived at the town of Atta, the ancestral hometown of the Chukwukas. It was in fact the reason the whole family had journeyed home that day. Most of the escapees from the murderous chaos in the north that had come back home to the Eastern region of Nigeria, had made their way home to their ancestral villages, where most of their families still resided.

The resulting strain of the appearance of hundreds of thousands of people back to the villages at such short notice, activated the communities to pitch together and offer whatever aid they could to their traumatized and often injured tribespeople.

Food, medicine, shelter and whatever was needed by the returnees, were put up by Igbo people everywhere for their friends and relatives. Meetings were called throughout the land at every level, trying to find out the direction the country was headed, in the aftermath of the bloody counter coup and the resultant pogroms.

Col Ojukwu, the man who had helped foil the January coup along with the now deceased Aguiyi Ironsi, was elevated by Ironsi shortly thereafter as Military Administrator of the Eastern Region and now with the murder of his Commander in Chief, was the most senior surviving Igbo military officer, and had the unenviable task of protecting the interests, lives and property of his tribesmen at that crucial point in the country's history.

Back home, Henry Chukwuka called his son and daughter in law to his obi, the central and most important building in the Igbo traditional compound, so that they could talk about the events going on in the country.

"I'm worried about the general direction this country seems to be headed in, and the uncertainty for the future." Uchechi's father said as all three sat alongside his wife Akunna, with solemn expressions on the faces of everyone.

"To bc frank with you, your mother and I have been thinking about this ever since the pogroms started." This said with a look towards his wife, who nodded quietly and sadly, with knowledge of what was to be said and the implications for the future of the family…

What Uchechi and Mary were thinking at the time, was that they too had been having discussions on the unfolding events in the country and watching with growing unease at the instability and unfathomable acts going on all around the country…

"We've been thinking that maybe it might be safer for the two of you to return to the United States. That it might be safer for you, especially with Uzoma being so young and vulnerable now."

"Papa." Uchechi replied. "Actually, Mary and I have spoken about this very thing earlier today, and for a few days in fact. I've asked her if she could go back to Boston with Uzoma…"

"And I said no." Mary interrupted. "How can I leave all of you now, and at this time? After all the time I've spent here. You are my family. I can't just leave and run when things are bad. How about Uzoma? How will he learn the language and know about his people, if he is far away in the United States?".

Listening to the impassioned plea from his wife as she addressed the family, Uchechi felt not just a sense of overwhelming love and pride in Mary, thinking that he had been quite probably the luckiest man alive. A foreign wife who was as passionate as any of his own tribespeople about the welfare of the people was rare, but at the same time he knew why his parents had called this meeting. All measures had to be considered to protect the vulnerable. Every avenue available to be used in the preservation of life, had to be explored.

"Mary" Uchechi's mum called to her daughter-in-law, speaking up for the first time since the opening greetings. "You know how much your father-in law and I dote after your child, our grandchild, the first Chukwuka born in this new generation. You have to understand how serious we consider the situation in the country, that we would even contemplate such an option."

"As it is, we are apprehensive for you to even go to Lagos." Her husband added. "Which is the seat of power for those murderous soldiers. But that's the only international airport. If anything happened to further push this country down the path to anarchy, and the way to Lagos proves to be hazardous to travel to, for you three as a family, your mother-in-law and I would never forgive ourselves."

The discussion continued on into the night, until Uzoma woke up from sleep, and Mary went to him to take him from Ngozi, Uchechi's only sister and her closest companion and gossip partner in the family, who had kept an eye on the sleeping Uzoma while the family meeting took place, on a topic that was being discussed across the extended family in hushed terms long before the night.

As he and Mary lay in bed that, both thinking of the discussion that had gone on earlier, Uchechi felt a wave of sadness and regret, for he could not yet bring himself to tell Mary just yet.

Once a decision was going to be made in the affirmative of Mary and Uzoma going back to the United States, he could not go with them. He needed both of them to be safe, but he could not also abandon his parents and siblings to the uncertainty of what might be a war.

He would never quite live with himself if anything happened to them while he was safe and hidden away in a foreign land. He suspected that Mary already knew that was what he might do, as she had always been able to read him so well and he her, an ever-present feature of the foundations of their love for one another. He wondered if it was partly the reason for her vehement refusal to go along with any plan requiring her to move back to the United States. She would be leaving so much behind, some not as obvious as others…

They continued to talk, as a family, on the events and policies emanating out of the military junta ruling the country, each event and policy pushing the nation slowly to the inevitability of a conflict amongst the regions, long after they had left Atta, but still Mary resisted the option to move to the safety of the U.S.

However, it was an unforeseen shock that finally led her to give in to the option of safety. As loyal as she was to Uchechi, and as wonderful as she had been to her new family and people, she was after all, a mother, and a young one at that, with a young child in tow.

A mother's instinct to protect her child at any cost supersedes all other considerations, and so when the horrible news came from the United States, followed by equally appalling news from Lagos, she finally relented to the pleas of her husband and in-laws.

For Uchechi, not being able to be in Lagos for his friend Chris, that human symbol of perfection for what it meant to be an Igbo man in the ever-developing world, when he was at his lowest and most vulnerable state, would live with him forever…

CHAPTER FOURTEEN

Uchechi looked at his friend lying down on his bed in obvious pain and did his best to hold back tears from falling down his face. He had to be strong, not just for Chris, but also for his wife Shirley, whom he had just barely been married to and who, in addition to sadness and confusion of her husband's condition, was adjusting to life in a foreign country without the help of her life partner to navigate through the terrain of Igbo culture and life.

Chris' parents, siblings and extended family were also present, and whilst he could see sad and downcast faces across the compound, there were no tears being shed, and he realized that they had all decided to show their support and radiate strength and hope to their stricken son, brother and relative.

But as he looked down towards his friend from the chair that had been pulled up for him in the small room where he lay down, all Uchechi could see in his mind's eye were the sporting memories of the great leopard of Eliot House. The goals, the unbelievable skill on the field, the incredible prowess on the track, and the celebrations of each one of his accomplishments by each astonished audience. The contrast from the recent past to the present was striking and for one longtime fan and friend, especially sad.

Chris Ohiri had been diagnosed with terminal lung cancer shortly after collapsing while playing a game of tennis in July at Cambridge just a few months before, at about the same time as the military junta in Nigeria were about to unleash their murderous campaign, thousands of miles and a continent away.

On learning the devastating news, Chris did what all Igbo people wish for should they know that their time on Earth was coming to an end, or what they would wish their family members would do for them should they pass away in a foreign land. He asked his newly married wife to accompany back to the land of his people. There was nothing more that could be done for him in America, and so he came home to see his family, rest and wait.

Being that he was Igbo, his re-entry to Nigeria via Lagos was at about the same time anti-Igbo sentiment was rife across the country, with tensions in the then capital being especially high with the junta operating out of Dodan Barracks in the city, Chris was detained and manhandled by the soldiers at the airport, wholly unsympathetic to the pleas of a dying man.

News of that detention came back east, and Uchechi's parents and Mary had to plead with him not to go out to Lagos to assist his friend on account of the dangerous climate for Igbo people. "What will you do when you get there?" Mary had asked. "You are a civilian going up against soldiers that will not hesitate to kill you, should you give them any excuse to. They haven't needed one so far!"

Uchechi would always feel a little shame, anytime he remembered that decision to not go to Lagos to help his friend. As he looked at his stricken friend, he could only imagine what it must have felt like to be in that situation, sick, helpless and alone.

"Hey Uche, why the long face?" Chris called to him, shaking him out of his afternoon reverie. "I hope you didn't come all this way to lead the singing of Hymn 210?" (The number of the popular burial hymn from the Ancient & Modern book of hymns, Rock of Ages).

"I've heard you sing before, and if you are here to sing anything, they might as well call me to heaven, right now."

The entire room immediately burst out in laughter, the solemness of the situation at hand temporarily forgotten. Uchechi's kept smiling even as the laughter died down. This was the Chris he had known and admired. The man who could light up any room, field or stadium. The man who could send an entire campus of students into celebrations, or an entire town and country. On any part of two continents. A man whose personality shone in every situation. Even one where the looming shadow of man's temporary presence in the world, permeated every inch of the room they were in.

Uchechi stayed at Chris's home until it was almost nighttime, talking and moving around the compound with his long-time friend, even venturing outside along with Shirley to see a mutual friend who had gone to Government College, even if it was a brief visit.

Shirley remarked to Uchechi that Chris looked so much stronger than he did earlier in the week, putting it down to his visit. "It's been a strange and lonely time here." She said, when Chris had gone out of the room to speak with a visitor.

“I don’t really know who to turn to and talk about all this. We had no idea that we would be coming back here at this time. Everything in the last few months has been a bit of a blur. I’m really glad you came. I think he needed you here for old time’s sake. Today, felt like we were back in Cambridge again, with old friends reminiscing about the things we cared about.”

“I wish I could have been with you two even earlier.” Uchechi replied. “But I’m glad I got the chance to see you again. There was a time we were worried if it was possible, after the shenanigans in Lagos. Next time, when I come over, I’ll bring Mary and our son Uzoma to see you. You do need the company. I know it isn’t easy, looking after Chris while getting used to the new community you’ve become a part of, but keep at it. We all need to be strong for Chris. He’s always been the strongest of us, the very best. The one who lifted everyone else. He just needs our help, this one time…”

Uchechi cried silently when he had gotten back home, after things had gotten quiet with Mary and Uzoma sleeping. It seemed only a short while ago, when he was walking down the streets of Cambridge with Chris, with people on either side of the road shouting felicitations on the occasion of yet another incredible display of physical prowess.

He just couldn't reconcile those memories, with the friend he had left earlier that day, quietly struggling to match his physical responses with the demands of his very astute mind, and he felt those struggles as much as he knew his friend did.

Mary accompanied him the next time he made the trip over to Chris' village. She had spoken to him the morning after his first trip to see their stricken friend. She never mentioned to him that she had overheard his hushed weeping the night before but encouraged him to tell her more about the visit than the precious little he had shared when he had arrived home. Once he opened up to her, she knew how serious Chris' condition was.

Shirley was grateful for the company, as well as the chance to get to see the barely 9-month-old Uzoma. Mary also brought over some American food she had bought before the trip down to Emekuku. Just as with

Uchechi's previous visit, they stayed until evening, having come down at midday, before leaving so they could get Uzoma home, cleaned up and in bed to rest from what was quite a busy day for him.

Chris had also been happy at the chance to see Uchechi's first born, but Uchechi himself felt a small sadness knowing that Chris would never get the chance to see a child of his own.

Uchechi kept visiting every week. Sometimes in the company of Mary, and at other times by himself. Every week, he noticed a bit more difficulty for his friend physically, and a bit more pain that Chris tried to keep hidden. But it was evident both on his face as well as that of Shirley. As time progressed, Chris would open up to his friend, not just about the difficulties presented from his daily fight with cancer, but also the future life battles that he would never have the opportunity to fight, to his great sadness.

The end came rather swiftly. Just five months after he was diagnosed in Cambridge with terminal lung cancer, he died on the 7th of November 1966. People came for the burial from far and wide. It might have been a few years since his exploits on the football field for the national team had so excited the area, but they all remembered, and came to send him home for the final time.

Emeka had actually come home from the U.S for the burial, once the arrangements had been made known, alongside Sarah. She along with Mary stayed next to Shirley all through the ceremony, giving her invaluable support in devastating times. Thereafter, Uchechi asked that she come spend some time in his place, just so she could continue to lean on the support provided by Mary, as well as Sarah who had stayed on for a while, whilst Emeka sorted through some family responsibilities.

As for Mary, the death of Chris was the final push she needed to heed the advice of Uchechi and his family to move back to the United States, even if it would be temporary. It wasn't just the details of the ordeal that Chris and Shirley had faced upon their re-entry into the country at the hands of the soldiers of northern origin, but in truth, more the sight of Shirley both during Chris's fight with terminal cancer, as well as her forlorn demeanor in the aftermath of her death.

She couldn't imagine, as much as she loved her in-laws, trying to raise Uzoma, and handle the intricacies of community life without Uchechi. And, if war was actually coming to the country, as all the signs seemed to suggest, she thought it best that they all leave to go back to Boston.

She convinced Shirley to stay around for just a bit longer, knowing the new widow was already planning to go back to the United States as she felt there was really no reason to stay in the country. Emeka's wife Sarah was also planning to go back as they had only planned on a visit of several weeks culminating with her first experience of Christmas as celebrated in Igboland.

Events of the next few weeks and months, however, would lead to changes in all their lives…

•

The pogroms in the north against the Igbo people hadn't just resulted in loss of life for thousands, but also lead to destruction of hundreds of businesses as well as the disruption in the activities of even more. The properties of the fleeing Easterners weren't spared either, whether it be houses, factories, vehicles of all kinds or the machines in factories. Anything that couldn't be stolen or confiscated, was burned.

This state of events meant that there was widespread disruption in business activities that specialized either in the movement of goods from Northern Nigeria down to the Southern parts or based in entirety in the north, most of which were owned by people of Igbo origin.

One of those businesses belonged to Mr. Onuoha, Emeka's father, who whilst a politician, had initially made his money from transportation, starting with a single lorry moving fresh farm produce and other stuff from North to South and vice versa and then gradually growing to a modest fleet as patronage and business opportunities grew.

In the last year, he had poured a huge amount of capital into the business in anticipation to meet the rising demand, as the country's population grew, for fresh farm produce and raw materials moved from the north to the markets and seaports down south.

It had an element of risk about it, being that he had decided to put his own money towards that investment, rather than try and secure bank loans. He was confident that with increased demand and opportunities for business growth in the country, the potential increase in revenue from his businesses would allow to recover and eventually make profit on his cash injection towards the venture.

Then, the countercoup of July '66 happened, and all his projections for growth were blown out of the water. His factories were looted and destroyed after the staff, mostly Igbos like him residing in the north for most of, if not all their lives, had been chased and had run for their lives.
His fleet of vehicles, now abandoned, were stolen, whilst those caught in operation were stopped and burnt in any part of the north they had been discovered in, due to the strong name recognition his company had gathered over the years.

The losses were devastating, and shortly after he fell ill. Word was sent to Emeka in New York, and he began making plans to come home to see his father, intimating Sarah on his plans and the serious nature of his dad's condition.

This being at the same time as Chris was going through the tragic final stages of life, Emeka and Sarah began the process of putting their affairs in order so that they could plan a visit towards the last weeks of the year and spend enough time with Emeka's family, and his father especially. That way, they would also be in a position to see Chris and spend time with him and Shirley, as the reports they were receiving from Uchechi showed a gradual downturn in their good friend's condition.

Of course, as it would turn out, they would never see Chris alive again, they just simply ran of time. So, when they got to Owerri, all they could do was pay their respects at his funeral and try to console the despondent Shirley.

Mr. Onuoha's health gradually declined as they approached Christmas, and barely a month after Chris' death, Emeka's dad died, in another tragically shocking surprise for the town that had just buried one of its most promising sons.

Emeka, being the first son, was now not only saddled with the task of burying his father, but also trying to hold together the family business that had been rapidly declining over the past few months, suffering from events that no one could have foreseen only six months prior.

This tragic turn of events forced Emeka into a painful decision. He had to stay back in Owerri and not go back with his beloved Sarah after his father's funeral, as he couldn't abandon family at this most critical juncture, massively disappointing Sarah, who whilst understanding his duty to family, had been hoping to start one of her own, with him.

Realizing that she would have to put those plans on hold and as ethnic tensions continued to rise in the country, she made plans to join Mary and Shirley on the trip back to the States, hoping that Emeka could sort out and stabilize the family business, and either join her again in New York, or get her to come visit him or stay in Owerri, once the tensions in the country had died down.

The wave to him, as she moved through the departure gates at the airport in Lagos, would be the last image she would see of her beloved Emeka…

•

Mary was making final plans for the family's departure to the United States that afternoon, she had already told her parents of their impending return, albeit temporary, having a talk with Shirley and Sarah on what dates they'd like to catch a flight in the new year, when Uchechi came into the room, having just come back from work, and beckoned to her for an aside once she had the chance.

"How was your day, baby?" Mary asked as soon as she had gotten the chance to leave her fellow Americans and give audience to Uchechi.

"It was okay. You can feel that everything is moving at snail's pace now. Nobody wants to invest or put much effort into anything, like they're expecting something calamitous to occur any moment. So, in reality, not much is happening. But there's something that has come up that we need to talk about."

"What's the matter? I hope nothing bad?" Mary asked anxiously, knowing the state of the country and the way tragic things had been happening amongst their circle of friends.

"It's Emeka. I've told you about how their family business has fallen on hard times, and how it will take a gargantuan effort and luck to pull it back from the brink? Well, he's asked for my help in getting the business back on track. He needs people he can trust right now, to help him with holding down the company assets, just so he knows for sure what he has left of the business. Just for a few months."

"What does this mean?" Mary asked, with a slight tone of anger and frustration creeping into her voice. "We've been planning our trip back to the States for weeks now. I mean, you asked that we go back because of the way things are going here. What do you want me to do now? Do you want me and Uzoma to stay back here? But it isn't safe. Or are you asking me to leave with Uzoma? That isn't fair. You said you would come with us. You can't tell me you're staying back here leaving me and the baby, just because your friend's business needs help? That makes no sense. None at all."

Uchechi moved closer to Mary, so that he was sitting on the arm of the chair where she sat and tried to take her hand, but she shrugged him off in obvious anger, to which he dragged a side stool around just so he could sit right in front of her, as he spoke.

"I've been meaning to tell you something for a while, Mary. I haven't said it because I wanted to mislead you, or go back on my word, or anything of the sort. I haven't said anything because I can't contemplate life without you and the son you've given me. You know you are my first and only girlfriend, the first and only girl I've fallen in love with, and outside of my family, the person I've spent the most time with, in my whole life. How could even think that I would ever want to be where you aren't?"

Gradually, Mary had let him take her hand, whilst looking him straight in the eyes as he spoke, knowing he meant every word. She then pulled even closer to him to ask him the question that had still not been answered and still troubled her.

"So why are you not coming with us back to Boston? Do you not like Boston? Or is staying with my parents? It was only going to be temporary. We could stay somewhere else if you like. I don't want you to stay here. If there is a war like they are saying might happen. This place won't be safe."

“That’s why I can’t come right now, my love. If anything happened to my family whilst I was safe in faraway America, I would never forgive myself, and if anything happened to you and Uzoma? I can’t even begin to imagine such a thing. The only way I can make sure everyone is safe, is to make you and Uzoma are away from danger in the U.S., then keeping an eye on the family just to be certain that they’ll be ok in the event of an outbreak of hostilities.”

“That’s fine Uche.” Mary said with sadness and resignation in her voice. “But’ who’s going to make sure that you are alright? You are making plans for everybody, but there are no plans to keep you safe. How am I sure, that the father of my son is going to keep safe and return to me?”

Uchechi got up from the side stool and knelt down in front of her with a kiss. “I promise that I’ll be back to be with you and Uzoma once things settle down. I just need to make sure the most important part of my life is safe. If you aren’t with me wherever I am, what on earth would I be doing there? Just trust me on this my love. I will come back to you in Boston.”

They stayed there in each other's arms until a cry from the bedroom alerted them that Uzoma had awoken from his afternoon nap. With a promise to talk some more later, Mary went in to get their son and bring him over to feed and play with his dad as he loved to do.

CHAPTER FIFTEEN

Uchechi sat at the back of the Peugeot Station wagon as it sped down the road from his hometown Atta, back towards the city of Owerri. People were everywhere, heading in all directions but mainly on foot.
There was a difference in tempo, with a surge in human activity and movement of people than Uchechi had noticed in the last three years.

No one was looking up at the sky, frantically looking out for planes trying to strafe unsuspecting and defenseless people going about the business of surviving a war. Maybe due to newfound lack of fear, there was a more relaxed stride by the women and children on the road, as they moved towards their various destinations.

Speaking of children, Uchechi was so glad that he hadn't seen signs of kwashiorkor amongst any of the children walking along the road that day. He had spent more than what seemed a lifetime, tending to and burying the kids afflicted by that terrible disease of malnutrition, brought on by the two- year government blockade of the sea from the breakaway Eastern region of Biafra, thereby stifling the movement of fish and other food rich in proteins and other essential nutrients.

Satisfying himself that the telltale signs were indeed not observable among those children, and that it was indeed safe to head back into the town of Owerri, Uchechi relaxed back into the seat of the vehicle transporting him and three other newly retired soldiers of the now defunct breakaway Republic of Biafra, and thought back to the incredible experience of the last years of the war of rebellion…

•

Mary and Uzoma had left, along with Shirley and Sarah for the United States in January 1967, after they had stayed to spend what already seemed at the time to be the last peaceful Christmas in the land of the Igbo.

The usual festive nature of the period was slightly muted in the knowledge of what had been arranged to happen in January. Uchechi and Mary spent every moment they could together, taking walks, going to the few places and towns in the land that they had wanted to go to, but had never quite gotten to visiting.

The nights were long and happy, then followed by mornings of inactivity as they knew they would be living on different continents in a short while, with no sure guarantees on when they would be reunited and living under one roof. But even worse was the unspoken knowledge they both had, that there wasn't a guarantee at all if they were actually going to be reunited, especially if things in Nigeria got even worse than they thought possible.

Once Mary and the ladies had safely reached the United States, Uchechi and Emeka got down to the task of securing the family business as requested by Emeka. With his younger brothers still in school, and too young to assist him in that crucial endeavor.

They went round to all the cities in the Eastern part of the country armed with inventory paperwork to places where Emeka's Dad had transport hubs, to recover what was left of his fleet of vehicles. Most of the time they were able to get hold of the assets at the location, but sometimes both the assets at the people supposed to look after the property were nowhere to be found. They would write off those assets, making a note to go back for a more thorough investigation, then hastily making their way to the next town on their list. They were aware that time was running against them. Just four months after Mary had left, the Republic of Biafra was formed in response to the Federal government's attempts to further isolate it and cut off its oil assets, with full blown war beginning in July.

Due to Uchechi's degree in Mechanical Engineering and Emeka's proficiency with his father's transport business, they were pulled into the 44th Electrical and Mechanical Engineer Battalion of the newly formed Biafran Army, under the command of Col Aghanya, a man who would go on to play a legendary part in the military achievements of the Biafran army throughout the war.

After some initial success against the massively superior numbers of the Federal troops, it became increasingly obvious that the new nation could not overcome Nigeria, no thanks to the massive military support from the United Kingdom, as it sought to secure its assets held in Nigeria, especially the Oil assets, which were almost all in the Eastern Region of the country, where the breakaway nation of Biafra was situated.

The British had never liked the Igbos, owing to the fact that they were the one ethnic group that fought the hardest and longest against the forced colonization of the area of West Africa that was later to be renamed Nigeria.
That historic conflict, that even went back as far the days of slavery, during which time the Igbos were known to be especially stubborn to the idea of being taken away as slaves, meant that the British always preferred their economic interests and assets to be controlled, or allowed access to, by the more subservient tribes in the country.

The realization that the war was only going to end one way, a slow but certain defeat for Biafra, if fought only by conventional means, lead to the radical idea to form a guerilla group to fight exclusively behind enemy lines, causing as much havoc as possible and massively disrupting the federal advance. This heroic group made up mainly civilian men and women, were trained and sent out to great success for the rest of the Nigerian Civil War.

They were nicknamed "The Rangers" but officially named the Biafra Organization of Freedom Fighters (BOFF), and Emeka in his capacity of knowing the back roads and area, owing to his experience with his father's transport business, frequently assisted the unit in its activities, by expediting their logistical needs.

It was on one of those missions in support of the Rangers during the offensive to recapture Owerri in January 1969, that Emeka was killed, with his body never to be recovered, as were so many other sons and daughters of Biafra during that terrible war.

Uchechi was the one to travel down to Mbaise, where the Onuoha family had gone once the war reached Owerri, to inform Emeka's mum of the demise of her first-born child, just two years after the sudden death of his father, only this time there would be no body to bury. Only mourning of the type Uchechi prayed never to witness again.

He made certain to go to Atta, where his parents and siblings had gone back to as conflict raged around Owerri, just to see if they were okay and also to quietly tell his dad, of the passing of the boy he had watched grow up to be a man. He made his father promise not to tell his mum of Emeka's passing until after he had left. He didn't think he could bear to listen to hear his mum half-ask him not to go back out there into the fray of battle, even though she knew he was out there to defend them all. She was after all, only human, and even more, a mother.

The war was a blur after that, with a constant prayer he offered to God every morning and every night, that he be allowed to keep the promise he had made to his wife and child, that he would be coming back over, to be with them once more.

So, when Owerri, which had become the new capital for Biafra once it had been recaptured, fell once again and for the final time in January of 1970, Uchechi, whilst sad that the promise of a new nation, free from its aggressors both within the continent and without, had failed to hold up in the face of monumental odds, thanked the God of his ancestors for preserving his life through the three years of brutal and tragic conflict.

The breeze that poured in from the open window of the Peugeot as it approached the federal checkpoints on the outskirts of Owerri, felt like release to the relaxed Uchechi, casually seated in the back seat.

The fact that the victorious and still dangerous Nigerian troops were going to have to give them access to a city he had always called home didn't bother him in the slightest. He was no longer in uniform and fortunately was not on the list of ex-Biafran military and civilians that were still being furtively hunted even though there had been a declaration of "No Victor, No Vanquished" when the Biafran surrender had been accepted.

At least God had allowed him to go home, something he knew only too well had not been possible for so many other men and women, none of them any less deserving that him…

•

It was evening when he finally got to what remained of his childhood neighborhood. He had strolled through the paths that he, Emeka and the rest of the gang used to walk down after school, joking and laughing at the intricacies and problems of secondary school life. If only they had known that those would be some of the best years of their lives…

Most of the houses along the road had been destroyed, and those left were in no condition to be considered habitable. There was no laughter to be heard anywhere in the vicinity, just what seemed like an audible sigh of relief that hung in the air, as if grateful that three years of pensive tension and horror were at an end.

Uchechi observed the environment as if for the first time, every compound where a home had once been, every side path leading to a different part of the neighborhood, or to another one entirely. The trees and flowers that were still by the side of the road and those weren't.

As he walked down the road, he imagined memories of the greatest friends that earth had bestowed on his childhood, laughing as if they were walking with him.

Chidi had remained in the United Kingdom after his studies and had simply stayed on when the war broke out, unable to safely return. I.K and Onyekachi had escaped to Ghana once the war started, so as not to have the anger of the Nigerian public fall on them whilst the war raged on in the east. As for the memories of Emeka and Chris…he hastened to where he had planned to visit all along, a bottle of palm wine firmly clutched under his left armpit as he walked solemnly down the road.

Reaching his destination, he walked into the favorite hideaway spot that he and Emeka had used when they were kids. The last time they had been they together was in the aftermath of the news that Uchechi had been selected to go to Harvard on the scholarship program, almost ten years earlier.

School, travel and life had made it so, that they had not had the opportunity to meet up again to fulfill the promise they had made to each other all those years ago. It was the thought that had kept coming into Uchechi's head as he wept on the way home that night, from telling Emeka's mum that her son was no more.

Time flies, the world turns, and we humans forget things, a lot of them simple things, easy promises to make in the beginning, but impossible to rectify when the opportunity to fulfill them passes us by…

Uchechi opened the bottle of palm wine and prayed for the souls of his friends and brothers in every sense of the word other than blood. Friends he would never get to see again, not even in memory on the faces of the children they would have made born Just like the life of the young hopeful nation that now lay in ruins, their promise had been extinguished too soon.

He poured a bit on the ground and called on the spirit of Chris to have his share, thanking him for all the memories and times they spent together, the pride that Chris' exploits at Harvard made him feel, proud to be Igbo in a foreign land, just as he was, where they had nothing as a standard for excellence other than themselves.
He apologized again for not always being by his side, as much as he could have been, and prayed that the great ancestors watch over him and keep him company until they met again, and for the God of his people to bless him in heaven as he had done for him whilst he walked the earth.

Another potion of wine was poured on the ground, and this time Uchechi called on his childhood friend Emeka to partake of his share. He prayed that he was well where he was, and that God would not hold it against him for partaking in the war to protect the people and to look after him in the afterlife. He also apologized for not being there for him at the end, and most importantly for not bringing his body back to the family for proper burial.

After sitting for a few minutes, taking a sip of wine in solidarity with the memories of two of the best men he had been blessed to meet with in life, he stood up and left the hideaway for the last time.

God had answered his prayers to keep him alive, and whilst time had indeed flown by, there was still a simple promise to be kept. Miracles are entirely the domain of God, but the desire to fulfill promises is much less empyrean.

There was a beautiful mother and a handsome son waiting on the fulfillment of a promise made, and as Uchechi made his way back up the road, he was glad of the opportunity to fulfill it…

FINAL THOUGHTS FROM THE AUTHOR

Whilst a lot of the characters in this book are fictional and others historically famous, there is one who is neither fictional nor as historically famous as he should be…at least not with his own people. But, with the sheer number of records and achievements he made in a short period of time in New England and throughout the Ivy League sports complex of the Northeastern United States in the early 60's, that shouldn't be possible.

He is not even remembered in Owerri where he grew up, the same town I grew up in after coming over from England as a child, about two decades after his time.

That should never be.

I discovered him when researching my book purely by accident, and resolved that in some fashion or another, I would tell the story of this young trailblazer, his uniqueness, bravery and sensational athletic prowess.

And yes, we are both Igbo, grew up in the same town and share the same birthday! Maybe, some things are destined to be…

Thankfully, he was not forgotten in the place he shone the most. Harvard University renamed their soccer grounds as Ohiri Field, in eternal honor of the student who brought over some much joy with him from a continent far away.

He was taken away from us too soon, at age 28.

R.I.P Chris Ohiri

IHEANYI ANUNUSO